IRISH TALES OF TERROR

GHOSTS, GHOULS AND GOBLINS FROM SOME OF IRELAND'S FINEST WRITERS

British Library Cataloguing-in-Publication Data
A catalogue record for this book is available from
the British Library

CONTENTS

THE DOOMED SISTERS
Charles Robert Maturin

* * *

The tranquillity of the Catholics of Ireland during the disturbed periods of 1715 and 1745 was most commendable, and somewhat extraordinary; to enter into an analysis of their probable motives is not at all the object of the writer of this tale, as it is pleasanter to state the fact of their honour than at this distance of time to assign dubious and unsatisfactory reasons for it. Many of them, however, showed a kind of secret disgust at the existing state of affairs, by quitting their family residences and wandering about like persons who were uncertain of their homes, or possibly expecting better from some near and fortunate contingency.

Among the rest was a Jacobite Baronet who, sick of his uncongenial situation in a Whig neighbourhood, in the north—where he heard of nothing but the heroic defence of Londonderry; the barbarities of the French generals; and the resistless exhortations of the godly Mr Walker, a Presbyterian clergyman to whom the citizens gave the title of 'Evangelist';—quitted his paternal residence, and about the year 1720 hired the Castle of Leixlip for three years (it was then the property of the Conollys, who let it to triennial tenants); and removed thither with his family, which consisted of three daughters—their mother having long been dead.

The Castle of Leixlip, at that period, possessed a character of romantic beauty and feudal grandeur, such as few buildings in Ireland can claim, and which is now, alas, totally effaced by the destruction of its noble woods; on the destroyers of which the writer would wish 'a minstrel's malison were said'. Leixlip, though about seven miles from Dublin, has all the sequestered and pictur-esque character that imagination could ascribe to a landscape a hundred miles from, not only the metropolis but an inhabited town. After driving a dull mile (an *Irish* mile) in passing from Lucan to Leixlip, the road—hedged up on one side of the high wall that bounds the demesne of the Veseys, and on the other by low enclosures, over whose rugged tops you have no view at all— at once opens on Leixlip Bridge, at almost a right angle, and displays a luxury of landscape on which the eye that has seen it even in childhood dwells with delighted recollection. Leixlip Bridge, a rude but solid structure, projects from a high bank of the Liffey, and slopes rapidly to the opposite side, which there lies remarkably low. To the right the plantations of the Veseys' demesne—no longer obscured by walls—almost mingle their dark woods in its stream, with the opposite ones of Marshfield and St Catharine's. The river is scarcely visible, overshadowed as it is by the deep, rich and bending foliage of the trees. To the left it bursts out in all the brilliancy of light, washes the garden steps of the houses of Leixlip, wanders round the low walls of its church-yard, plays with the pleasure-boat moored under the arches on which the summer-house of the Castle is raised, and then loses itself among the rich woods that once skirted those grounds to its very brink. The contrast on the other side, with the luxuriant vegetation, the lighter and more diversified arrangement of ter-raced walks, scattered shrubberies, temples seated on pinnacles, and thickets that conceal from you the sight of the river until you are on its banks, that mark the character of the grounds which are now the property of Colonel Marley, is peculiarly striking.

Visible above the highest roofs of the town, though a quarter of a mile distant from them, are the ruins of Confy Castle, a right good old predatory tower of the stirring times when blood was shed like water; and as you pass the bridge you catch a glimpse of the waterfall (or salmon-leap, as it is called) on whose noon-day lustre, or moonlight beauty, probably the rough livers of that age when Confy Castle was 'a tower of strength', never glanced an eye or cast a thought as they clattered in their harness over Leixlip Bridge, or waded through the stream before that convenience was in existence.

Whether the solitude in which he lived contributed to tranquil-lise Sir Redmond Blaney's feelings, or whether they had begun to rust from want of collision with those of others, it is impossible to say, but certain it is that the good Baronet began gradually to lose his tenacity in political matters; and except when a Jacobite friend came to dine with him, and drink with many a significant 'nod and beck and smile, the King over the water—or the parish priest (good man) spoke of the hopes of better times, and the final suc-cess of the *right* cause, and the old religion—or a Jacobite servant was heard in the solitude of the large mansion whistling 'Charlie is my darling', to which Sir Redmond involuntarily responded in a deep bass voice, somewhat the worse for wear, and marked with more emphasis than good discretion—except, as I have said, on such occasions, the Baronet's politics, like his life, seemed passing away without notice or effort. Domestic calamities, too, pressed sorely on the old gentleman: of his three daughters, the youngest, Jane, had disappeared in so extraordinary a manner in her child-hood, that though it is but a wild, remote family tradition, I cannot help relating it.

The girl was of uncommon beauty and intelligence, and was suffered to wander about the neighbourhood of the castle with the daughter of a servant, who was also called Jane, as a *nom de caresse*. One evening Jane Blaney and her young companion went far and deep into the woods; their absence created no uneasiness at the time, as these excursions were by no means unusual, till her playfellow returned home alone and weeping, at a very late hour. Her account was that, in passing through a lane at some distance from the castle, an old woman, in the *Fingallian* dress (a red petticoat and a long green jacket), suddenly started out of a thicket, and took Jane Blaney by the arm: she had in her hand two rushes, one of which she threw over her shoulder, and giving the other to the child, motioned to her to do the same. Her young companion, terrified at what she saw, was running away, when Jane Blaney called after her—'Good-bye, good-bye, it is a long time before you will see me again.' The girl said they then dis-appeared, and she found her way home as she could. An inde-fatigable search was immediately commenced—woods were traversed, thickets were explored, ponds were drained—all in vain. The pursuit and the hope were at length given up. Ten years afterwards, the housekeeper of Sir Redmond, having remembered that she left the key of a closet where sweetmeats were kept on the kitchen-table, returned to fetch it. As she approached the door, she heard a childish voice murmuring—'Cold—cold—cold how long it is since I have felt a fire!' She advanced, and saw, to her amazement, Jane Blaney, shrunk to half her usual size, and covered with rags, crouching over the embers of the fire. The housekeeper flew in terror from the spot, and roused the servants, but the vision had fled. The child was reported to have been seen several times afterwards, as diminutive in form as though she had not grown an inch since she was ten years of age, and always crouching over a fire, whether in the turret-room or kitchen, complaining of cold and hunger, and apparently covered with rags. Her existence is still said to be protracted under these dismal circumstances, so unlike those of Lucy Gray in Wordsworth's beautiful ballad:

> Yet some will say, that to this day
>   She is a living child—
> That they have met sweet Lucy Gray
>   Upon the lonely wild;
> O'er rough and smooth she trips along,
>   And never looks behind;
> And hums a solitary song
>   That whistles in the wind.

The fate of the eldest daughter was more melancholy, though less extraordinary; she was addressed by a gentleman of competent fortune and unexceptionable character: he was a Catholic, moreover; and Sir Redmond Blaney signed the marriage articles, in full satisfaction of the security of his daughter's soul, as well as of her jointure. The marriage was celebrated at the Castle of Leixlip; and, after the bride and bridegroom had retired, the guests still remained drinking to their future happiness when suddenly, to the great alarm of Sir Redmond and his friends, loud and piercing cries were heard to issue from the part of the castle in which the bridal chamber was situated.

Some of the more courageous hurried upstairs; it was too late— the wretched bridegroom had burst, on that fatal night, into a sudden and most horrible paroxysm of insanity. The mangled form of the unfortunate and expiring lady bore attestation to the mortal virulence with which the disease had operated on the wretched husband, and died a victim to it himself after the involuntary murder of his bride. The bodies were interred, as soon as decency would permit, and the story hushed up.

Sir Redmond's hopes of Jane's recovery were diminishing every day, though he still continued to listen to every wild tale told by the domestics; and all his care was supposed to be now directed towards his only surviving daughter. Anne, living in solitude, and partaking only of the very limited education of Irish females of that period, was left very much to the servants, among whom she increased her taste for superstitious and supernatural horrors, to a degree that had a most disastrous effect on her future life.

Among the numerous menials of the Castle there was one 'withered crone' who had been nurse to the late Lady Blaney's mother, and whose memory was a complete *Thesaurus terrorum*. The mysterious fate of Jane first encouraged her sister to listen to the wild tales of this hag, who avouched that at one time she saw the fugitive standing before the portrait of her late mother in one of the apartments of the Castle, and muttering to herself—'Woe's me, woe's me! how little my mother thought her wee Jane would ever come to be what she is!' But as Anne grew older she began more 'seriously to incline' to the hag's promises that she could show her her future bridegroom, on the performance of certain ceremonies which she at first revolted from as horrible and impious; but, finally, at the repeated instigation of the old woman, consented to act a part in. The period fixed upon for the performance of these unhallowed rites was now approaching—it was near the 31st of October, the eventful night when such ceremonies were, and still are supposed, in the North of Ireland, to be most potent in their effects. All day long the Crone took care to lower the mind of the young lady to the proper key of submissive and trembling credulity, by every horrible story she could relate; and she told them with frightful and supernatural energy. This woman was called *Collogue* by the family, a name equivalent to Gossip in England, or Cummer in Scotland (though her real name was Bridget Dease); and she verified the name by the exercise of an unwearied loquacity, an indefatigable memory, and a rage for communicating and inflicting terror that spared no victim in the household, from the groom, whom she sent shivering to his rug,

6

to the Lady of the Castle, over whom she felt she held unbounded sway.

The 31st of October arrived—the Castle was perfectly quiet before eleven o'clock; half an hour afterwards, the Collogue and Anne Blaney were seen gliding along a passage that led to what is called King John's Tower, where it is said that monarch received the homage of the Irish princes as Lord of Ireland, and which, at all events, is the most ancient part of the structure. The Collogue opened a small door with a key which she had secreted about her, and urged the young lady to hurry on. Anne advanced to the postern, and stood there irresolute and trembling like a timid swimmer on the bank of an unknown stream. It was a dark autumnal evening; a heavy wind sighed among the woods of the Castle, and bowed the branches of the lower trees almost to the waves of the Liffey which, swelled by recent rains, struggled and roared amid the stones that obstructed its channel. The steep descent from the Castle lay before her, with its dark avenue of elms; a few lights still burned in the little village of Leixlip—but from the lateness of the hour it was probable they would soon be extinguished.

The lady lingered. 'And must I go alone?' said she, foreseeing that the terrors of her fearful journey could be aggravated by her more fearful purpose.

'Ye must, or all will be spoiled,' said the hag, shading the miserable light, that did not extend its influence above six inches on the path of the victim. 'Ye must go alone—and I will watch for you here, dear, till you come back, and then see what will come to you at twelve o'clock.'

The unfortunate girl paused. 'Oh! Collogue, Collogue, if you would but come with me. Oh! Collogue, come with me, if it be but to the bottom of the castle-hill.'

'If I went with you, dear, we should never reach the top of it alive again, for there are them near that would tear us both in pieces.'

'Oh! Collogue, Collogue—let me turn back then, and go to my own room—I have advanced too far, and I have done too much.'

'And that's what you have, dear, and so you must go further, and do more still, unless, when you return to your own room, you would see the likeness of *some one* instead of a handsome young bridegroom.'

The young lady looked about her for a moment, terror and wild hope trembling at her heart—then, with a sudden impulse of supernatural courage, she darted like a bird from the terrace of the Castle, the fluttering of her white garments was seen for a few moments, and then the hag who had been shading the flickering light with her hand, bolted the postern and, placing the candle before a glazed loophole, sat down on a stone seat in the recess of the tower, to watch the event of the spell. It was an hour before the young lady returned; when her face was as pale, and her eyes as fixed, as those of a dead body, but she held in her grasp *a dripping garment*, a proof that her errand had been performed. She flung it into her companion's hands, and then stood panting and gazing wildly about her as if she knew not where she was. The hag herself grew terrified at the insane and breathless state of her victim, and hurried her to her chamber; but here the preparations for the terrible ceremonies of the night were the first objects that struck her and, shivering at the sight, she covered her eyes with her hands, and stood immovably fixed in the middle of the room.

It needed all the hag's persuasions (aided even by mysterious menaces), combined with the returning faculties and reviving curiosity of the poor girl, to prevail on her to go through the remaining business of the night. At length she said, as if in desperation, 'I *will* go through with it: but be in the next room; and if what I dread should happen, I will ring my father's little silver bell which I have secured for the night—and as you have a soul to be saved, Collogue, come to me at its very first sound.'

The hag promised, gave her last instructions with eager and jealous minuteness, and then retired to her own room, which was adjacent to that of the young lady. Her candle had burned out, but she stirred up the embers of her turf fire, and sat nodding over them, and smoothing her pallet from time to time, but resolved not to lie down while there was a chance of a sound from the lady's room, for which she herself, withered as her feelings were, waited with a mingled feeling of anxiety and terror.

It was now long past midnight, and all was silent as the grave throughout the Castle. The hag dozed over the embers till her head touched her knees, then started up as the sound of the bell seemed to tinkle in her ears, then dozed again, and again started as the bell appeared to tinkle more distinctly—suddenly she was roused, not by the bell, but by the most piercing and horrible cries from the neighbouring chamber. The Crone, aghast for the first time at the possible consequences of the mischief she might have occasioned, hastened to the room. Anne was in convulsions, and the hag was compelled reluctantly to call up the housekeeper (removing meanwhile the implements of the ceremony), and assist in applying all the specifics known at that day, burnt feathers, etc., to restore her. When they had at length succeeded, the housekeeper was dismissed, the door was bolted, and the Collogue was left alone with Anne; the subject of their conference might have been guessed at, but was not known until many years afterwards; but Anne that night held in her hand, in the shape of a weapon with the use of which neither of them was acquainted, an evidence that her chamber had been visited by a being of no earthly form.

This evidence the hag importuned her to destroy, or to remove, but she persisted with fatal tenacity in keeping it. She locked it up, however, immediately, and seemed to think she had acquired a right, since she had grappled so fearfully with the mysteries of futurity, to know all the secrets of which that weapon might yet lead to the disclosure. But from that night it was observed that her character, her manner, and even her countenance, became altered. She grew stern and solitary, shrank at the sight of her former associates, and imperatively forbade the slightest allusion to the circumstances which had occasioned this mysterious change.

It was a few days subsequent to this event that Anne, who after dinner had left the Chaplain reading the life of St Francis Xavier to Sir Redmond, and retired to her own room to work and, perhaps, to muse, was surprised to hear the bell at the outer gate ring loudly and repeatedly—a sound she had never heard since her first residence in the Castle; for the few guests who resorted there came and departed as noiselessly as humble visitors at the house of a great man generally do. Straight way there rode up the avenue of elms, which we have already mentioned, a stately gentleman, followed by four servants, all mounted, the two former having pistols in their holsters, and the two latter carrying saddle-bags before them: though it was the first week in November, the dinner hour being one o'clock, Anne had light enough to notice all these circumstances. The arrival of the stranger seemed to cause much, though not unwelcome tumult in the Castle; orders were loudly and hastily given for the accommodation of the servants and horses—steps were heard traversing the numerous passages for a full hour—then all was still; and it was said that Sir Redmond had locked with his own hand the door of the room where he and the stranger sat, and desired that no one should dare to approach it. About two hours afterwards, a female servant came with orders from her master to have a plentiful supper ready by eight o'clock, at which he desired the presence of his daughter. The family establishment was on a handsome scale for an Irish house, and Anne had only to descend to the kitchen to order the roasted chickens to be well strewed with brown sugar according to the unrefined fashion of the day, to inspect the mixing of a bowl of sago with its allowance of a bottle of port wine and a large handful of the richest spices, and to order particularly that the pease pudding should have a huge lump of cold salt butter stuck in its centre; and then, her household cares being over, to retire to her room and array herself in a robe of white damask for the occasion. At eight o'clock she was summoned to the supper-room. She came in, according to the fashion of the times, with the first dish; but as she passed through the ante-room, where the servants were holding lights and bearing the dishes, her sleeve was twitched, and the ghastly face of the Collogue pushed close to hers; while she muttered 'Did not I say *he would come for you*, dear?' Anne's blood ran cold, but she advanced, saluted her father and the stranger with two low and distinct reverences, and then took her place at the table. Her feelings of awe and perhaps terror at the whisper of her associate were not diminished by the appearance of the stranger; there was a singular and mute solemnity in his manner during the meal. He ate nothing. Sir Redmond appeared constrained, gloomy and thoughtful. At length, starting, he said (without naming the stranger's name), 'You will drink my daughter's health?' The stranger intimated his willingness to have that honour, but absently filled his glass with water; Anne put a few drops of wine into hers, and bowed towards him. At that moment, for the first time since they had met, she beheld his face—it was pale as that of a corpse. The deadly whiteness of his cheeks and lips, the hollow and distant sound of his voice, and the strange lustre of his large, dark, moveless eyes, strongly fixed on her, made her pause and even tremble as she raised the glass to her lips; she set it down, and the with another silent reverence retired to her chamber.

There she found Bridget Dease, busy in collecting the turf that burned on the hearth, for there was no grate in the apartment. 'Why are you here?' she said, impatiently.

The hag turned on her, with a ghastly grin of congratulation. 'Did not I tell you that *he* would come for you?'

'I believe he has,' said the unfortunate girl, sinking into the huge wicker chair by her bedside; 'for never did I see mortal with such a look.'

'But is not he a fine stately gentleman?' pursued the hag.

'He looks as if he were not of this world,' said Anne.

'Of this world, or of the next,' said the hag, raising her bony forefinger, 'mark my words – so sure as the (here she repeated some of the horrible formularies of the 31st of October) so sure he will be your bridegroom.'

'Then I shall be the bride of a corpse,' said Anne; 'for he I saw tonight is no living man.'

A fortnight elapsed, and whether Anne became reconciled to the features she had thought so ghastly, by the discovery that they were the handsomest she had ever beheld—and that the voice, whose sound at first was so strange and unearthly, was subdued into a tone of plaintive softness when addressing her—or whether it is impossible for two young persons with unoccupied hearts to meet in the country, and meet often, to gaze silently on the same stream, wander under the same trees, and listen together to the wind that waves the branches, without experiencing an assimilation of feeling rapidly succeeding an assimilation of taste; or whether it was from all these causes combined, but in less than a month Anne heard the declaration of the stranger's passion with many a blush, though without a sigh. He now avowed his name and rank. He stated himself to be a Scottish Baronet, of the name of Sir Richard Maxwell; family misfortunes had driven him from his country, and for ever precluded the possibility of his return: he had transferred his property to Ireland, and purposed to fix his residence there for life. Such was his statement. The courtship of those days was brief and simple. Anne became the wife of Sir Richard, and, I believe, they resided with her father till his death, when they removed to their estate in the North. There they remained for several years, in tranquillity and happiness, and had a numerous family. Sir Richard's conduct was marked by but two peculiarities: he not only shunned the intercourse, but the sight of any of his countrymen, and, if he happened to hear that a Scotsman had arrived in the neighbouring town, he shut himself up till assured of the stranger's departure. The other was his custom of retiring to his own chamber, and remaining invisible to his family on the anniversary of the 30th of October. The lady, who had her own associations connected with that period, only questioned him once on the subject of this seclusion, and was then solemnly and even sternly enjoined never to repeat her inquiry.

Matters stood thus, somewhat mysteriously, but not unhappily, when on a sudden, without any cause assigned or assignable, Sir Richard and Lady Maxwell parted, and never more met in this world, nor was she ever permitted to see one of her children to her dying hour. He continued to live at the family mansion, and she fixed her residence with a distant relative in a remote part of the country. So total was the disunion, that the name of either was never heard to pass the other's lips, from the moment of separation until that of dissolution.

Lady Maxwell survived Sir Richard forty years, living to the great age of 96; and, according to a promise, previously given, disclosed to a descendant with whom she had lived, the following extraordinary circumstances.

She said that on the night of the 30th of October, about seventy-five years before, at the instigation of her ill-advising attendant, she had washed one of her garments in a place where four streams met, and performed other unhallowed ceremonies under the direction of the Collogue, in the expectation that her future husband would appear to her in her chamber at twelve o'clock that night. The critical moment arrived, but with it no lover-like form. A vision of indescribable horror approached her bed, and flinging at her an iron weapon of a shape and construction unknown to her, bade her 'recognise her future husband by *that*.' The terrors of this visit soon deprived her of her senses; but on her recovery, she persisted, as has been said, in keeping the fearful pledge of the reality of the vision which, on examination, appeared to be incrusted with blood. It remained concealed in the inmost drawer of her cabinet till the morning of her separation. On that morning, Sir Richard Maxwell rose before daylight to join a hunting party. He wanted a knife for some accidental purpose and, missing his own, called to Lady Maxwell, who was still in bed, to lend him one. The lady, who was half asleep, answered, that in such a drawer of her cabinet he would find one. He went, however, to another, and the next moment she was fully awakened by seeing her husband present the terrible weapon to her throat, and threaten her with instant death unless she disclosed how she came by it. She supplicated for life, and then, in an agony of horror and contrition, told the tale of that eventful night. He gazed at her for a moment with a countenance which rage, hatred, and despair converted, as she avowed, into a living likeness of the demon-visage she had once beheld (so singularly was the fated resemblance fulfilled), and then exclaiming, 'You won me by the devil's aid, but you shall not keep me long,' left her—to meet no more in this world. Her husband's secret was not unknown to the lady, though the means by which she became possessed of it were wholly unwarrantable. Her curiosity had been strongly excited by her husband's aversion to his countrymen, and it was so stimulated by the arrival of a Scottish gentleman in the neighbourhood some time before, who professed himself formerly acquainted with Sir Richard, and spoke mysteriously of the causes that drove him from his country, that she contrived to procure an interview with him under a feigned name, and obtained from him the knowledge of circumstances which embittered her after-life to its latest hour. His story was this:

Sir Richard Maxwell was at deadly feud with a younger brother; a family feast was proposed to reconcile them, and as the use of knives and forks was then unknown in the Highlands, the company met armed with their dirks for the purpose of carving. They drank deeply; the feast, instead of harmonising, began to inflame their spirits; the topics of old strife were renewed; hands, that at first touched their weapons in defiance, drew them at last in fury, and in the fray, Sir Richard mortally wounded his brother. His life was with difficulty saved from the vengeance of the clan, and he was hurried towards the sea-coast, near which the house stood, and concealed there till a vessel could be procured to convey him to Ireland. He embarked *on the night of the 30th of October*, and while he was traversing the deck in unutterable agony of spirit, his hand accidentally touched the dirk which he had unconsciously worn ever since the fatal night. He drew it, and, praying 'that the guilt of his brother's blood might be as far from his soul as he could fling that weapon from his body', sent it with all his strength into the air. This instrument he found secreted in the lady's cabinet, and whether he really believed her to have become possessed of it by supernatural means, or whether he feared his wife was a secret witness of his crime, has not been ascertained, but the result was what I have stated.

The reparation took place on the discovery: for the rest,

I know not how the truth may be,
I tell the Tale as 'twas told to me.

THE CHILD WHO LOVED A GRAVE

Fitz-James O'Brien

*   *   *

Far away in the deep heart of a lonely country there was an old
solitary churchyard. People were no longer buried there, for it
had fulfilled its mission long, long ago, and its rank grass now fed
a few vagrant goats that clambered over its ruined wall and roamed
through the sad wilderness of graves. It was bordered all round
with willows and gloomy cypresses; and the rusty iron gate, seldom
if ever opened, shrieked when the wind stirred it on its hinges
as if some lost soul, condemned to wander in that desolate
place forever, was shaking its bars and wailing at the terrible
imprisonment.

In this churchyard there was one grave unlike all the rest. The
stone which stood at the head bore no name, but instead the
curious device, rudely sculptured, of a sun uprising out of the sea.
The grave was very small and covered with a thick growth of dock
and nettle, and one might tell by its size that it was that of a little
child.

Not far from the old churchyard a young boy lived with his

parents in a dreary cottage; he was a dreamy, dark-eyed boy, who never played with the children of the neighbourhood, but loved to wander in the fields and lie by the banks of rivers, watching the leaves fall and the waters ripple, and the lilies sway their white heads on the bosom of the current. It was no wonder that his life was solitary and sad, for his parents were wild, wicked people who drank and quarrelled all day and all night, and the noises of their quarrels where heard in calm summer nights by the neighbours that lived in the village under the brow of the hill.

They boy was terrified at all this hideous strife, and his young soul shrank within him when he heard the oaths and the blows echoing through the dreary cottage, so he used to fly out into the fields where everything looked so calm and pure, and talk with the lilies in a low voice as if they were his friends.

In this way he came to haunt the old churchyard, roaming through its half-buried headstones, and spelling out upon them the names of people that had gone from earth years and years ago. The little grave, nameless and neglected, however, attracted him more than all others. The strange device of the sun uprising out of the sea was to him a perpetual source of mystery and wonder; and so, whether by day or night, when the fury of his parents drove him from his home, he used to wander there and lie amidst the thick grass and think who was buried beneath it.

In time his love for the little grave grew so great that he adorned it after his childish fashion. He cleared away the docks and the nettles and the mulleins that grew so sombrely above it, and clipped the grass until it grew thick and soft as the carpet of heaven. Then he brought primroses from the green banks of dewy lanes where the hawthorn rained its white flowers, and red poppies from the cornfields, and bluebells from the shadowy heart of the forest, and planted them around the grave. With the supple twigs of the silver osier he hedged it round with a little simple fence, and scraped the creeping mosses from the grey head-stone until the little grave looked as if it might have been the grave of a good fairy.

Then he was content. All the long summer days he would lie upon it with his arms clasping its swelling mound, while the soft wind with wavering will would come and play about him and timidly lift his hair. From the hillside he heard the shouts of the village boys at play, and sometimes one of them would come and

17

ask him to join in their sports; but he would look at him with his calm, dark eyes and gently answer no; and the boy, awed and hushed, would steal back to his companions and speak in whispers about the child that loved a grave.

In truth, he loved the little graveyard better than all play. The stillness of the churchyard, the scent of the wild flowers, the golden chequers of the sunlight falling through the trees and playing over the grass were all delights to him. He would lie on his back for hours gazing up at the summer sky and watching the white clouds sailing across it, and wondering if they were the souls of good people sailing home to heaven. But when the black thunder-clouds came up bulging with passionate tears, and bursting with sound and fire, he would think of his bad parents at home, and, turning to the grave, lay his little cheek against it as if it were a brother.

So the summer went passing into autumn. The trees grew sad and shivered as the time approached when the fierce wind would strip them of their cloaks, and the rains and the storms buffet their naked limbs. The primroses grew pale and withered, but in their last moments seemed to look up at the child smilingly, as if to say, 'Do not weep for us. We will come again next year.' But the sadness of the season came over him as the winter approached, and he often wet the little grave with his tears, and kissed the grey head-stone, as one kisses a friend that is to depart for years.

One evening towards the close of autumn, when the woods looked brown and grim, and the wind as it came over the hills had a fierce, wicked growl, the child heard, as he was sitting by the grave, the shriek of the old gate swinging upon its rusty hinges, and looking up he saw a strange procession enter. There were five men. Two bore between them what seemed to be a long box covered with black cloth, two more carried spades in their hands, while the fifth, a tall stern-faced man clad in a long cloak, walked at their head. As the child saw these men pass to and fro through the graveyard, stumbling over half-buried head-stones, or stooping down and examining half-effaced inscriptions, his little heart almost ceased to beat, and he shrank behind the grey stone with the strange device in mortal terror.

The men walked to and fro, with the tall one at their head, searching steadily in the long grass, and occasionally pausing to consult. At last the leader turned and walked towards the little grave, and stooping down gazed at the grey stone. The moon had just risen, and its light fell on the quaint sculpture of the sun rising out of the sea. The tall man then beckoned to his companions. 'I have found it,' he said, 'it is here.' With that the four men came along, and all five of them stood by the grave. The child behind the stone could no longer breathe.

The two men bearing the long box laid it down in the grass, and taking off the black cloth, the child saw a little coffin of shining ebony covered with silver ornaments, and on the lid, wrought in silver, was the device of a sun uprising out of the sea, and the moon shone over all.

'Now to work!' said the tall man; and straightaway the two that held the spades plunged them into the little grave. The child thought his heart would break; and, no longer able to restrain himself, he flung his body across the mound, and cried out to the strange leader.

'Oh, Sir!' he cried, sobbing, 'do not touch my little grave! It is all I have to love in the world. Do not touch it; for all day long I lie here with my arms about it, and it seems like my brother. I tend it, and keep the grass short and thick, and I promise you, if you will leave it to me, that next year I will plant about it the finest flowers in the meadows.'

'Tush, child, you are a fool!' answered the stern-faced man. 'This is a sacred duty that I have to perform. He who is buried here was a child like you; but he was of royal blood, and his ancestors dwelt in palaces. It is not meet that bones like his should rest in common soil. Across the sea a grand mausoleum awaits them, and I have come to take them with me and lay them in vaults of porphyry and marble. Take him away, men, and to your work.'

So the men dragged the child from the grave by main force, and laid him nearby in the grass, sobbing as if his heart would break; and then they dug up the grave. Through his tears he saw the small white bones gathered up and put in the ebony coffin, and heard the lid shut down, and saw the men shovel back the earth into the empty grave, and he felt as if they were robbers. Then they took up the coffin and retraced their steps. The gate shrieked once more on its hinges, and the child was alone.

He returned home silent, and tearless, and white as any ghost. When he went to his little bed he called his father, and told him he was going to die, and asked him to have him buried in the little

19

grave that had a grey head-stone with a sun rising out of the sea carved upon it The father laughed, and told him to go to sleep; but when morning came the child was dead!

They buried him where he wished; and when the sod was patted smooth, and the funeral procession departed, that night a new star came out in heaven and watched above the grave.

THE PORTRAIT OF ROISIN DHU

Dorothy Macardle

*   *   *

It was a year after the artist was drowned that the loan exhibition
of Hugo Blake's paintings was opened in Philadelphia by Maeve.
'Whom the gods love die young,' people said.

To remember those paintings is like remembering a dream-life
spent with the Ever-living in an Ireland untrodden by men.

Except once he never painted a human face or any form of life,
human or fairy, yet the very light and air of them thrilled with
life—it was as though he had painted life itself. There was the great
'Sliav Gullion'—stony, austere—the naked mountain against the
northern sky, and to look at it was to be filled with a young, fierce
hunger for heroic deeds, with the might of Cuchulain and Fionn.
There was 'Loch Corrib' like a mirage from the first day of
Creation—there was Una's 'Dawn' . . .

The critics, inarticulate with wonder, made meaningless phrases:
'Blake paints as a seer,' 'He paints on the astral plane.'

At the end of the room, alone on a grey wall, hung the 'Portrait
of Roisin Dhu'. Before her, Irish men and women stood worship-
ping, the old with tears, the young with fire in their eyes. There
were men whom it sent home.

Had Blake seen, anywhere on earth, others were asking, that
heart-breaking, entrancing face? Knowledge of the secrets of God
was in the eyes; on the lips was the memory, the endurance and
the foreknowledge of endless pain; yet from the luminous, serene
face shone out a beauty that made one crave for the spaces beyond
death.

No woman in the world, we said, had been Hugo's Roisin
Dhu; no mortal face had troubled him when he painted that

immortal dream—that ecstasy beyond fear, that splendour beyond anguish—that wild, sweet holiness of Ireland for which men die.

Maeve, as we knew, had been his old friend. When strangers clamoured, 'Was there a woman?' she would not tell. But one evening when we were five only around Una's fire she told us the strange, incredible tale.

'I will not tell everyone for a while,' she said, 'because so few would understand, and Hugo, unless one understood to the heights and depths, might seem to have been . . . unkind. But I will tell you: There was a girl.'

'It is almost impossible to believe,' Liam said; 'It is not a human body he has painted; nor even a human soul!'

'That is true in a way,' Maeve answered, hesitating; 'I will try to make you understand.

'He was the loneliest being I have ever known. He was a little atom of misery and rebellion when my godmother rescued him in France. She bought the child from a drunkard who was starving him almost to death. His mother, you know, was Nora Raftery, the actress; she ran away from her husband with François Raoul, taking the child, and died. Poor Blake rode over a precipice while hunting—mad with grief, and the boy was left without a friend in the world. It was I who taught him to read and write: already he could draw.

To the end he was the same passionate, lonely child. The anguish of pity and love he had had for his mother he gave to her country when he came home: he suffered unbearable 'heim-weh' all the years he was studying abroad. The 'Dark Tower' as we called it, of our godmother's house on Loch Corrib was the place he loved best.

I have known no one who lived in such extremes, always, of misery or of joy. In any medium but paint he was helpless— chaotic or dumb, yet I think that his pictures came to him first not visually at all, but as intense perceptions of a *mood*. And between that moment of perception and the moment when it took form and colour in his mind he used to be like a wild creature in pain. He would prowl day and night around the region he meant to paint, waiting in a rage of impatience for the right moment of light and shadow to come, the incarnation of the soul . . . Then, when he had found it, the blessed mood of contentment would come

23

and he would paint, day after day, until it was done. At those times, in the evenings, he would be exhausted and friendly and grateful like a child.

For all the vehemence that you feel in his work he painted very slowly, with intense, exquisite care, like a man in love. That is indeed what he was—in love, obliviously, with whatever spirit had enthralled his imagination at the time. And when the picture was finished and the vision gone he fell into a mood of desolation in which he wanted to die. He was very young.

I tried to scold Hugo out of those moods. I was with him in April just after he had finished his 'Loch Corrib'—you know the innocence, the angelic tranquillity in it, like the soul of a child. He would not go near the lake: 'It is nothing to me now,' he said sombrely, 'I have done with it.'

'Hugo!' I said, laughing, 'you are a vampire! The loch has given you its soul.' He answered, 'Yes: that is true; corpses are ugly things.'

For a month that empty, dead mood lasted and Hugo hated all the world. I took him to London to give him something to hate. After two days he fled back to his tower and breathed the smell of the peat and sea-wind, and the sweet, home-welcome of burning turf, and looked out on Ireland with eyes of love. The next morning he came in from a bathe in the loch with the awakened, wondering look I had longed to see and said, 'I am going to paint Roisin Dhu.' Then he went off to walk the west of Ireland seeking a woman for his need.

I was astonished and excited beyond words; he had been so contemptuous of human subjects, although I remembered, in his student days, studies for heads and hands that had made one artist whisper, 'Leonardo!' under his breath.

I wondered what woman he would bring home.

They came about two weeks later, after dark, rowing over the loch, Hugo and the girl alone.

After supper, sitting over the turf fire in the round hall of the tower, Hugo told me that she was the daughter of a king.

She smiled at him, knowing that he spoke of her although she had no English at all, and I told her in Irish what he had said. She answered gravely, 'It is true.'

I looked at her then as she moved from the window to her chair, and I felt almost afraid—her beauty was so delicate and so remote . . .

'Those red lips with all their mournful pride' . . . Poems of Yeats were haunting me while I looked at her. But it was the beauty of one asleep, unaware of life or of sorrow or of love . . . the face of a woman whose light is hidden . . .

She sat in the shadowed corner, brooding, while Hugo talked. He was at his happiest, overflowing with childish delight in his achievement and with eagerness for tomorrow's sun.

Nuala was her name. The King of the Blasket Isles was her father—a superstitious, tyrannical old man. Hugo had been able to make no way with him or his sons.

'I invited one of them to come too, and take care of her,' he said, 'but they would not hear of it at all.

'The old man was as dignified as a Spanish Grandee.

' "It is not that I would be misdoubting you, honest man," says he, "but my daughter is my daughter and there is no call for her to be going abroad to the world."

'And her brothers was as obstinate:

' " 'Tis not good to be put in a picture: it takes from you," they said.'

'They got me into a boat by a ruse, rowed me "back to Ireland", and when they had landed me pulled off.

' "The blessing of God on your far travelling!" they called to me gravely: a hint that I would not be welcome to the island again.

'You can imagine the frenzy I was in!' he said. And I could, well. He had walked night after night on the rocks of the mainland planning some desperate thing, but one night Nuala came to him, rowed out through the darkness by some boys who braved the vengeance of the old king for her sake. He rewarded them extravagantly and brought Nuala home.

He told it all triumphantly, and Nuala looked up at him from time to time with a gentle gaze full of content and rest. But my heart sank: there was only one possible end to this; Hugo, at his best, was loving and kind and selfless—all might be well—but I knew my Hugo after work.

She slept in my room and talked to me, softly, in the dark, asking me questions about Hugo's work. 'He told me you were his sister-friend,' she said.

I told her about his childhood, his suffering and his genius: she listened and sighed.

'It is a pity of him to be so long lonely,' she said, 'but he will not be lonely any more.'

'Why, Nuala?' I asked, my heart heavy with dread for her. Her answer left me silent.

'I myself will be giving him love.'

Hugo had found a being as lost to the world as himself. How would it end for her, I wondered. She slept peacefully, but I lay long awake.

The next morning work began in the studio at the top of the tower. I gave up all thought of going home. Nuala would need me.

Hugo was working faster than usual it seemed, beginning as soon as the light was clear and never pausing until it failed. I marvelled at Nuala's endurance, but I dared not plead for her. I had wrecked a picture of Hugo's once by going into his studio while he painted: his vision fled from him at the least intrusion and I had learned to keep aloof.

Day after day, when they came down at last to rest and eat, I could measure his progress by the sombre glow of power in his eyes. I could imagine some young druid when his spells proved potent, looking like that.

But the change that came over Nuala frightened me; he was wearing her away: her face had a clear, luminous look, her eyes were large and dark; I saw an expression in them sometimes as of one gazing into an abyss of pain. The change that might come to a lovely woman in years, seemed to come to her in days: the beauty of her, as she sat in the candle-light, gazing at her own thoughts in the shadows, would still your breathing. It grew more wonderful, more tragic, from day to day.

One night after she had stolen away to bed, exhausted, while Hugo sat by the fire in a kind of trance, I forced myself to question him.

'Hugo,' I said, as lightly as I could, with my heart throbbing: 'Is it that you are in love with your Roisin Dhu?'

He looked up suddenly, with a dark fire in his eyes. 'Love,' he whispered in a voice aching with passion. He rose and threw back his head and cried out in tones like deep music—

'I could plough the blue air!
I could climb the high hills!

O, I could kneel all night in prayer
To heal your many ills!'

Then he sighed and went away.

Nuala's look was becoming, day by day, a look of endurance and resignation that I could not bear, as of one despairing of all human happiness yet serene.

At last I questioned him again:

'Will you be marrying your Roisin Dhu?'

He turned on me startled, with a laugh, both angry and amazed.

'What a question! What an outrageous question, Maeve!'

I was unanswered still.

When seven weeks had gone I grew gravely anxious. I feared that Nuala would die: she had the beauty you could imagine in a spirit new-awakened from death, a look of anguish and ecstasy in one . . . She was frail and spent; she scarcely spoke to me or seemed to know me; she slept always in the garden alone.

It was towards the end of June that I said to Hugo, 'You are wearing your model out.'

'I am painting her better than God created her,' he answered. Then he said, contentedly, 'I shall have done with her very soon.'

I cannot express the dread that fell on me then; I was torn with irresolution. To interfere with Hugo—to break the spell of his vision, would not only sacrifice the picture, it might destroy him. I thought his reason would not survive the laceration, the passion that would follow the shattering of that dream.

That night I found Nuala utterly changed. She came down from the studio dull-eyed and ugly and went straight to bed in my room.

Hugo told me he did not want her any more.

I rowed her out next morning across the loch: it was one of those grey, misty days when it is loveliest; the Twelve Bens in the distance looked like mountains of Hy Breasail, the weeds and sedges glimmering silvery-gold . . . but she had no eyes for its beauty, no beauty of her own, no light . . . she lay drowsy and unresponsive on her cushions; her hands and face were like wax.

I would have rebelled that night, taken any risk, to make Hugo undo what he had done. She lay down to sleep under a willow by the water's edge and I went to him in the hall. He was standing by the fire and turned to me as I came in; there was a look of wondering humility in his face, as if his own achievement were a thing to worship—a thing he could not understand.

'Tomorrow!' he said: 'It will be finished in an hour: you shall see it.' Then he came and took my hands in his old, affectionate way and said:

'You have been such a good sister-friend!'

One hour more! She must endure it: I would not sacrifice him for that. But I lay awake all night oppressed with a sense of fear and cruelty and guilt.

At breakfast time there was no Hugo: he had eaten and started work. Old Kate rang the bell in the garden but Nuala did not come. My fears had vanished with the sweet air and sunshine of the early morning: larks were singing; it was mid-June: the joy of Hugo's triumph was my own joy. I went down to the willow where I had left Nuala asleep. She was lying there still; she never stirred when I touched her. She was cold.

I called no one, I ran madly up the spiral stair to Hugo's studio in the tower. Outside his door I paused: the memory of the last time I had broken in and the devastating consequences arrested me even then. I pushed the door open without a sound and stood inside, transfixed.

I looked for a moment and grew dizzy, so amazing was the thing I saw. Hugo stood by his easel: before him on the dais, glimmering in the misty silver light, stood Nuala, gazing at him, all a radiance of consummated sacrifice and sweet, unconquerable love—Nuala, as you have seen her in the portrait of Roisin Dhu.

Hugo stumbled, laid down his brush, drew his hand over his eyes, then turned and, seeing me, said, 'It is done.'

When I looked again at the dais she was gone.

I was shaken to the heart with fear. I cried out, 'Come to her! She is dead.'

He ran with me down to the water's edge.

I believe I had hoped that he would be able to waken her, but she was cold and dead, lying with wide-open eyes.

Hugo knelt down and touched her, then rose quickly and turned away: 'How unbeautiful!' he said.

I called out to him sternly, angrily, and he looked down at her again, then stooped and lifted her in his arms.

'Maeve, Maeve!' he cried then, piteously: 'Have I done this?'

He brought her home with state to the Island, told them she

had been his bride and gave her such a burial as the old King's heart approved. Then he came home again to his lonely house. I left it before he came; he had told me he wanted to be alone.

I heard nothing of him then for a long time and felt uneasy and afraid. After I had written many anxious letters a strange, disjointed answer came.

'She has never left me,' he wrote. 'She is waiting, near, quite near. But what can I do? This imprisoning body—this suffocating life—this burdenous mortality—this dead world.

'The picture is for you, Sister-friend, and for Ireland when you die.'

Before I could go to him the picture came and with it the news that he was drowned.

They found the boat far out on the loch.'

Maeve's face was pale when she ended: she covered her eyes for a moment with her hand.

'He had seen the hidden vision . . .' one of us said.

Nesta was looking into the fire, her dark eyes wide with foreboding.

'It is written in Destiny,' she said: 'the lovers of Roisin Dhu must die.'

DANSE MACABRE
L. A. G. Strong

* * *

'Tell me,' said Mr Mangan, 'do you dance?'

'Seldom,' I answered. 'They discourage me.'

'Who discourage ye?'

'My female relatives.'

Mr Mangan made no comment on this. Evidently he was not interested in my performance, and had only raised the subject in order to introduce some reminiscence of his own.

'Now, you are an observant man, too damned observant I think sometimes. Did you ever observe old Flanagan?'

'You mean the shopkeeper down there in the village?'

'Yerra, who else would I mean?'

Mr Mangan filled his pipe and lit it.

Some thirty years ago—he said—that same Flanagan was the handsomest-looking young divil, the most indefatigable sower of wild oats, in ten parishes. He dressed to distraction, he spent like a lord, and half the girls in the place were crazy about him. He laughed from morning to night, he danced like a puma, you saw him at every race-meeting, aye, and he was lucky too. It was a series of solid wins that set him up in the hardware business.

One night we'd a Red Cross dance above in the school. Mrs Mangan and I were there in our official capacity, and there was young Flanagan, in a six-guinea suit and gloves, and bedamn, it was a treat to see him. He danced with a dozen different girls, and there were their mothers, sitting over against the walls, like old pike watching a school of innocent young migratory frogs.

We'd a kind of a bar rigged up where the schoolmaster usually presides, with ices, mineral waters, tea, and such. As for the intelligentsia, all they had to do was to sneak out of the back door and up the lane into the 'Coach and Horses'.

Mrs Mangan was dispensing at the bar, and I seemed to be achieving little except getting in young people's way, when sud-

31

denly I noticed a new face. I thought I knew everyone in the room, but this particular city-bred-looking piece of feminine fragility seemed a new-comer. I find it hard to describe her, except that she had a Burne-Jones look—pre-Raphaelite—you know, the sort that the lachrymose artists of that time loved to depict floating on their back in green swamps, or streeling by the dozen up interminable staircases dressed in limp nightshirts.

This girl wore a long gauze sort of a frock with a necklace of imitation pearls. She had golden shoes on, with high heels, and to tell you the truth I thought she looked a bit out of date. She was leaning against the far end of the bar counter, and she seemed breathless, though I hadn't noticed her dancing.

I made my way along to the wife.

'Who's that pretty girl?' I asked her. 'The one with the yellow frock. Look—over there.'

Mrs Mangan took one look and went on serving out the tea.

'Listen to me,' she said, out of the side of her mouth. 'This is a highly respectable dance. It's been got up in aid of the Red Cross, and not for the benefit of the "Coach and Horses".'

Well, there were too many people around, and I couldn't argue with her. But for the moment she gave me quite a turn, as she often can.

However, I was sober all right, I know that. The girl was there in front of me; she was no hallucination. I resolved to go and speak to her, ask if she was enjoying herself, or could I get her something. I hoped the wife would see me, too. It would serve her right.

Before I could get to the girl, however, young Flanagan swept down on her with a flash and a smile, and before you could say snipe he had her swirling around to the strains of the 'Destiny' waltz.

I watched them going round the floor, the girl and young Flanagan, he laughing and talking and bending over her, and she half-responding, but with a sort of a look—I thought maybe it was my fancy—as if it wasn't of this night she was thinking, but of other nights long past, other partners, other waltzes. It's hard to be sure, afterwards, what you remember and what you put in from later knowledge.

Towards the end of the evening I was busy with my official duties, and couldn't keep an eye on them. I didn't see them again till the dance was done. There were but two motor-cars in the place then, and one of them still survives—Sheehy the baker's. The other belonged to Flanagan, a red, noisy, rackety affair which he got second-hand in town for seventy-five pounds. As I left the school-room, after putting out the lights, I saw Flanagan, and the lady beside him, crash off in the car with a sound of guns and thunder, and he with his handsome head thrown back, roaring with laughter.

Do ye know the road from here to town? Ye do? Then ye'll know the little cemetery, perched on the top of the hill: a few tombstones and a rusty iron gate. You may have wondered in your innocence why that spot was chosen for a graveyard. Rural economy, me boy. There's little to be got by ploughing and growing swedes or potatoes on a stony hill, but sure, it'll be a handy spot for a take-off when Gabriel blows his horn.

Well—to come back to Flanagan. I didn't see him for ten days or a fortnight after the dance. I heard afterwards he went on a jag up in town, and it was over a week before he came back, with no red car. It must have been the father and mother of a jag, I thought, for he seemed to have sobered up for good. He bought the shop where he is now, and settled down very seriously to business. But it didn't look to be doing him much benefit: before the year was out everyone was talking about the change in his appearance. His hair was greying, indeed it was going white on him; his face was yellow and wrinkled like a turkey's neck, his good looks fled before your eyes, and faith, now that financially he was a real sound catch, it seemed plain that he was safe from matrimony for ever.

After he'd been settled down into a busy confirmed shopkeeper for two or three years he became one of four typhoid cases we had in the village, the only cases we ever had that I remember. Aye, and he was the only one who survived. The sickness didn't improve his looks, as you can believe.

Listen now to what I'm going to tell ye. Ye know Mrs Mangan, and ye'll know I'm speaking without prejudice when I say that she's never so happy as when she's helping some poor divil who can't help himself. Well, Flanagan was over the killing part of the sickness, but he was very feeble, he'd no one to tend him, and it didn't look as if he'd stay the course. So Mrs Mangan persuaded him to come to our place and lie about and convalesce; and she got a cousin of hers, a lad with a red beard as long as your arm, who'd been in the grocery business and made a packet and retired to enjoy it, only being a miserable sort of a divil he didn't enjoy anything very much—she persuaded this boyo to come and look after Flanagan's business while he was laid by. By the same token, the cousin got rid of four gross of tin plates that had been duds with Flanagan ever since he opened the place. The long bearded lad sent them away, had them enamelled white, then splattered the whole window with them at sixpence apiece, and bedad in a week there wasn't one left.

But Flanagan. The wife fed him like a prize-fighter, and after six weeks he was able to be up and out and taking the air in my donkey-and-trap. The donkey got more exercise than he was used to or indeed tolerated, and yet he grew fat as a barrel. I couldn't make it out. Then I found Flanagan used to buy carrots and apples and sugar-sticks for his trips, and feed the donkey.

One autumn night, we were sitting in front of the fire, the wife and I and Flanagan, with his big forgetting eyes staring into last year. There'd been something in the paper about a fire at a dance hall, and all of sudden the wife speaks to him, without looking up from her sewing.

'Tell me, Mr Flanagan,' says she. 'I've often wondered. Mangan here had a story of you driving away, after that last Red Cross dance we had, with a pretty girl in yellow. He insists that he pointed her out to me at the time, but, faith, I thought he'd been to the "Coach and Horses".'

Flanagan had gone stiff as she spoke. Then he relaxed and let a long sigh out of him.

'I'm glad you asked me that, Mrs Mangan. It'll be a relief to tell someone. Oh yes, she was with me all right. I danced several dances with her. She was queer and absent, but she excited me, she was different from any other girl I'd met. At first she was so vague and elusive, I wondered, God forgive me, I wondered if her vagueness came from some young man's hip pocket. I asked her name and address, and she gave me them: Maud Gillie was the name, and an address in—well, never mind the address.

'I was smitten and piqued: I wasn't used to being treated in this offhand way, and when the dance was over I asked might I drive her home. Yes, she said, yes; just like that; more of a shrug of the shoulders.

'I tucked her up in my rug, and we set off. She didn't speak. When we'd driven maybe ten minutes in the white moonlight, at the top of the hill there, at Finstown, a bit short of the graveyard, she turned to me. "Let me down here," she said.

'We're not home yet, I said. I thought she was half asleep. "Let me down, please," she repeated. What? I said. Here, by the old graveyard? "Let me down at once," she said, "or I'll go."

'I pulled up, there was such strain in her voice. Maybe she was feeling ill, I thought. We were right by the graveyard gate. I jumped out, and hurried round to open the door for her and let her out. For three seconds, maybe, I had my eyes off her. You won't believe me, either of you—but when I got round to open the door, the car was empty.'

Mrs Mangan and I stared at him. I felt my spine creep.

'Empty,' he said. 'There was the seat, cold, filled with moonlight. I looked around, Not a sign or sound. Maud Gillie had gone. Disappeared. Evaporated.

'I don't know how long I stood there, like a frozen man. Silence. Clear, cold moonlight. I think I must have lost my head. I told myself there was an explanation. I jumped back into the car, and drove like mad to town. I drove to the address she'd given me, and pulled the bell, but there was no answer. Almost out of my mind, I looked for an hotel. I found one, ill lit. I parked the car outside, I got a bed. Did I sleep? Faith I did not. I tossed and tumbled and shivered the night through.

'Morning came, and a fine dismal rain, the rain you get at a funeral. I could eat no breakfast. As soon as I decently could, I went out and came to Maud Gillie's house. I rang, and rang, and I knocked. At last a slatternly girl opened the door, but she showed no disposition to let me in. While we parleyed on the step, an elderly woman came down the hall. She was dressed in faded and shabby black, with a sort of filmy wrap round her neck.

'"Well," she said, "and what do you want, young man, at this hour of the morning?"

'"You are Mrs Gillie, ma'am, are you?"

'"I am. And what of it, pray?"

'Then I told her about the dance, and how I'd started to drive her daughter home, and had somehow lost her.

'"She made me let her down there, at Finstown, by the grave-yard, ma'am. I couldn't find her again. I was terribly anxious. I—

I came to see if in some miraculous way she had got home."

'I backed away then, for the grim old woman had advanced till her chest was almost touching my own. Her face was convulsed and terrifying. She gave a shrill, thin squeal, like a rabbit caught by a stoat.

'"Get out of this, you infernal young blackguard!" she cried.

'"Ma'am! ma'am!" I backed down the steps. "I'm sorry. I only came to inquire was your daughter all right."

'"All right? All right?"

'She came out after me, and stood on the top step. I could see the drizzle falling against her black dress.

'"The fine daughter she was, with her dances and her gallivantings. I told her she'd pay for it. She was killed, you young fool, killed in a drunken car crash, and I buried her in that cemetery at Finstown. Now get out of here, or I'll call the police.'

'I fled,' said Flanagan to us. 'I sold the car, and spent the money in a way I'm bitterly ashamed of: but I had to try to forget, or I'd have lost my reason, I think. Look at my hair, Mrs Mangan. You see what that night did for me. I was never the same after it.

'Well, I'm glad to have told you both. You've been the soul of kindness to me. I'm nearly well again now. I'll be able to relieve your cousin next Monday, Mrs Mangan, I hope. And now, if you'll excuse me, I'll go up to my bed.'

'He went up,' said Mr Mangan, 'and he left the two of us staring at each other across the fireplace. Well—you'll come to the dance next week, won't you?'

THE UNBURIED LEGS

Gerald Griffin

In the cool grey of a fine Sunday morning in the month of June,
Shoresha Hewer, dressed out in a new *shoot* of clothes, and with
a pair of runner leather brogues that had never been on the foot
of man before, set out from his father's little cabin, romantically
situated amidst a little group of elder and ash trees, on the banks
of the river Flesk, to overtake an early mass in the village of
Abbeydorney. Such, at least, to the old couple, was represented
as the ostensible object of Shoresha's long walk, though they did
not fail to hint to one another, with half-suppressed smiles, as he
closed the door after him, that his views were not altogether
limited to that sacred ceremony. What was really uppermost in
his thoughts on that auspicious morning, as he brushed along with
a light and springing step over heather or tussock—whether the
chapel, where he was to kneel by the side of a little blue-eyed,
fair-haired devotee, during the service, and the long and digressive
exhortation; or the barn at Abbeydorney cross, where he was to
commence the evening dance with her, it would be invidious
to scrutinise, and was especially of little consequence on this
occasion, as both his love and his devotion fell prostrate before a
master-feeling which suddenly usurped an absolute command over
the events of the day.

As he was trudging along a low monotonous heath-covered
country, whistling the old air of *Thau me en a hulla agus na dhusig
me,* he came to a high double ditch, covered with blackthorn
bushes, with here and there the decaying trunk of an old oak or
beech, throwing forth a few weakly shoots, which still waved their

* I am asleep, and don't wake me.

slender boughs in the wind, as if almost in mimicry of the mighty arms it once stretched forth over the fields. He looked along the bank, and observing a spot where the ascent was likely to prove easy, caught hold of a branch to assist him in mounting, when he heard a noise at the other side, and a rustling among the bushes, as if someone was making his way through; he got his foot, however, on a tuft of rushes in the ditch side to proceed, when suddenly with a loud exclamation he tumbled backward into the field; for what should he see walking upon the top of the ditch, and just preparing to jump down, but two well-shaped, middle-sized legs, without either hip, body, or head. It was just as if they had been cut off a little above the knee, and though there was nothing to connect or regulate their movements, they climbed, jumped and progressed along the moor, in as well adjusted steps as if the first dancing-master of the county of Kerry had been superintending their movements. They evidently belonged to a man, as appeared not only from their figure and size, but from the portion of the white kerseymere garment which buckled at the knee, over a neat silk stocking. The shoes were square-toed, of Spanish leather, and were ornamented with old-fashioned silver buckles, such as had not been used in that part of the country for some generations. They had slowly paced by Shoresha, and already left him staring behind, at the distance of a good stone-throw, before he recovered from his astonishment sufficiently to think of rising, which he accomplished slowly, and almost involuntarily, never taking his eyes off the legs, but ejaculating to himself, 'Blessed mother in heaven! is it awake or dreaming I am?' They had now got on so far, that he perceived they would be soon out of sight if he did not move in pursuit; so abandoning Abbeydorney and its inducements, he, without hesitation, adopted that resolution.

It would be vain to detail all the ohs! the Dhar a dieus! the monoms! that escaped from Shoresha, time after time, as the legs hopped over a trench, picked their steps through a patch of bog, or pushed through a thicket. He was before long joined by a neighbour who was on his way to Listowel, for the priest to christen his child, but who could not resist the temptation of following and ascertaining how this extraordinary phenomenon should end. A smith, and a little boy who had been despatched to fetch him from the cross-road by a traveller to get a few nails driven into a loosened shoe, soon after fell in with them. A milkmaid laid down her can and spancill, and some ragged gorçoons gave over their early game of goal, as they came up, and so great were the numbers collected when they approached Listowel, even at that dewy hour of the morning, that it seemed like the congregation of some little village chapel moving along at prayer time.

It was amusing enough, when they arrived at the waters of the Flesk, to observe with what delicacy and elegance the legs tripped over it, from stepping stone to stepping stone, without getting spot or speck on the beautiful silk stockings. They now cut across the country at a nimble gait, the procession behind lengthening every hour, and increasing in clamorous exclamations of wonder as it proceeded.

After some hard walking, they descended into a wooded glen, where the tangled underwood, and wild briar, and close and stooping branches of the older timber, rendered it no pleasant travelling to such as were under the heavy disadvantage of a superincumbent body. To the subjects of our narrative, which were annoyed by no such lumber, of course no difficulties presented themselves; they hopped over the dense brushwood, or ducked under the branchy arms of oak or elm stretched across the path, with equal activity, while the most eager of the crowd behind were eternally knocking their foreheads and noses against some unobserved bough, or dragging their tattered clothes through blackthorn and briar: several, wearied and fretted with the chase, soon fell behind, while others, seeing no probability of any immediate termination to it, and altogether ignorant to what it might lead, gave up in apprehension. A thousand surmises about it were already afloat; some saying, they saw them going to stop once or twice, and that they certainly would not go much farther; others swearing out, that ''twas faster and faster they were walking every moment, and that the dickens a one of 'em would stop or stay until they got to the banks of the Shannon.' Many suggested that it wasn't they at all that were there, but only, as it were, the shapes of 'em; and that they'd keep going, going, ever, until it was night, and lead 'em all into some wood or desert place; and then, maybe, the ground to open beneath 'em, or a gust of wind to come by and sweep 'em away in one *gwall*, so that they'd never be heard of after. The legs had, meantime, crossed a shallow part of the river Gale that stole noiselessly through the bottom of the glen, and pressed on with renewed vigour at the opposite side. A flat, moorish, uninteresting looking country fell fast behind them; and, as they invariably pursued the most direct route to Tarbert, the tired followers, which now consisted chiefly of boys and young men, began in good earnest to suspect that town to be their real destination. They were, however, soon relieved from these disagreeable anticipations, when the legs arrived opposite a place called Newtownsands, made a sudden stop, wheeled the toes round to the right, and almost instantly sprang across a little trench; they then advanced rapidly towards the remains of an old church, which are still to be seen there, within one or two fields of the road. There are but three roofless walls now standing; and close to where the west gable formerly stood is one solitary tree which, in that unwooded and almost uninhabited region, only adds to the universal loneliness. There are a few graves about, but even these are only observable on a very close approach, so buried are they in the long rank grass and weeds, and in the fallen rubbish of the building. To one of these, which lay close to the south wall, our heroes moved on, but at a more measured, and it would seem, reverential pace than before; and kneeling slowly down beside it, remained in that position before the wondering eyes of the few who had persevered in the pursuit, and had now, one after another, come up. As their courage grew in contemplating the pacific and holy attitude of the legs, they began gradually to contract their circle, and creep nearer and nearer; but the closer they approached, the more shadowy did the objects become, until the resemblance was only to be distinguished by a fleecy, almost transparent outline, which moment after moment was less defined, and at last melted away into thin air.

Such was the story that occupied the thoughts and tongues of all the gossips from Newtownsands to Abbeydorney, for months and years after. As the occurrence was in itself quite unique in its kind, even those who pretended to the most intimate communication with the spiritual world, as well as the confessed and best accredited agents of the *gentlemen*, were wholly unable to offer anything like a probable explanation of it. One old blind woman, who was, indeed, the Lord knows how old, and was wrinkled and grey in the memory of the baldest inhabitant of Abbeydorney, called to mind a tale that had been told her when a child, which perhaps may be said to give some clue to it.

'There lived,' she said, 'in former times, a lady of immense wealth, who had a strong castle not far from Abbeydorney, though no one could now tell where; and two great lords came to propose for her: one a fair-haired, blue-eyed youth, of a delicate make and graceful manner; the other a dark, stout, athletic figure, but proud and uncourtly. The lady liked the fair lad best, which made the other so jealous of him that he was determined, one way or another, to compass his death. So he engaged a fellow, by a large sum of money, to get access to his bedroom at night, and cut off his head with a hatchet. On the night the murder was to be committed, he made the lad, who never suspected him, drink more wine than usual after dinner, that he might be wholly incapable of resistance. In this state he retired to his room, where he threw himself on the bed without undressing, and, as it awkwardly enough happened, with his head towards the bed's feet. In a few minutes, in came the fellow with the hatchet, and struck a blow that he thought must have severed the head from the body, but it was the two legs he had cut off. Upon this the young lord groaned, and immediately after received another blow, which killed him. The corpse was put into a sack and carried that night to Newtownsands, where it got Christian burial; but the legs were thrown into a hole in the castle garden, and covered up with earth. The lord who had procured the murder, the next day pretended to the lady that the blue-eyed lad had returned home; upon which, not knowing the deceit, she became quite offended, and in a few weeks after agreed to marry his rival. But in the midst of the joy and feasting on the bridal night, there was a horn blown outside the castle, and soon after, steps were heard ascending the grand staircase, and the doors of the bridal-hall flew open, and in walked two bodyless legs. Then there was screaming, and running, and the bride fainted; but the legs followed the bridegroom about everywhere, until he quitted the castle; and it was said that wherever he looked or turned to, from that hour, he saw them stalking before, or beside, or behind him, until he wasted and fell into a decay. And when he was dying he confessed the whole, and desired the assassin might be searched for everywhere, to ascertain from him where the legs were thrown, that they might be dug up, and get Christian burial; but the villain was never found from that day to this, and maybe,' continued the old woman, 'the legs are in punishment this way, and get leave to walk the country of an odd time, to show what's happening to them, and make some good soul search them out, and have them removed to Newtownsands.'

THE MAN FROM SHORROX'

Bram Stoker

*　　*　　*

'Throth, yer 'ann'rs, I'll tell ye wid pleasure; though, trooth to tell, it's only poor wurrk telling the same shtory over an' over agin. But I niver object to tell it to rale gintlemin, like yer 'ann'rs, what don't forget that a poor man has a mouth on to him as much as Creeshus himself has.

'The place was a market-town in Kilkenny—or maybe King's County, or Queen's County. At all events, it was wan of them counties what Cromwell—bad cess to him!—gev his name to. An' the house was called after him that was the Lord Liftinint an' invinted the polis—God forgive him! It was kep' be a man iv the name iv Misther Mickey Byrne an' his good lady—at laste it was till wan dark night whin the bhoys mistuk him for another gintle-man, an unknown man, what had bought a contagious property— mind ye the impidence iv him. Mickey was comin' back from the Curragh Races wid his skin that tight wid the full of the whisky inside of him that he couldn't open his eyes to see what was goin' on, or his mouth to set the bhoys right afther he had got the first tap on the head wid wan of the blackthorns what they done such

44

jobs wid. The poor bhoys was that full of sorra for their mishap whin they brung him home to his widdy that the crather hadn't the hearrt to be too sevare on thim. At the first iv course she was wroth, bein' only a woman afther all, an' weemin not bein' gave to rayson like min is. Millia murdher! but for a bit she was like a madwoman, and was nigh to have cut the heads from aff av thim wid the mate chopper, till, seein' thim so white and quite, she all at wance flung down the chopper an' knelt down be the corp.

'"Lave me to me dead," she sez. "Oh min! it's no use more people nor is needful bein' made unhappy over this night's terrible wurrk. Mick Byrne would have no man worse for him whin he was living, and he'll have harm to none for his death! Now go; an', oh bhoys, be dacent and quite, an' don't thry a poor widdied sowl too hard!"

'Well, afther that she made no change in things ginerally, but kep' on the hotel jist the same; an' whin some iv her friends wanted her to get help, she only sez:

'"Mick an' me run this house well enough; an' whin I'm thinkin' of takin' help I'll tell yez. I'll go on be meself, as I mane to, till Mick an' me comes together agin.'

'An', sure enough, the ould place wint on jist the same, though, more betoken, there wasn't Mick wid his shillelagh to kape the pace whin things got pretty hot on fair nights, an' in the gran' ould election times, when heads was bruk like eggs—glory be to God!

'My! but she was the fine woman, was the Widdy Byrne! A gran' crathur intirely: a fine upshtandin' woman, nigh as tall as a modherate-sized man, wid a forrm on her that'd warrm yer hearrt to look at, it sthood out that way in the right places. She had shkin like satin, wid a warrm flush in it, like the sun shinin' on a crock iv yestherday's crame; an' her cheeks an' her neck was that firrm that ye couldn't take a pinch iv thim—though sorra wan iver dar'd to thry, the worse luck! But her hair! Begor, that was the finishing touch that set all the min crazy. It was just wan mass iv red, like the hearrt iv a burnin' furze-bush whin the smoke goes from aff iv it. Musha! but it'd make the blood come up in yer eyes to see the glint iv that hair wid the light shinin' on it. There was niver a man, what was a man at all at all, iver kem in be the door that he didn't want to put his two arrms round the widdy an' giv' her a hug immadiate. They was fine min too, some iv thim—and warrm

45

men—big graziers from Kildare, and the like, that counted their cattle be scores, an' used to come ridin' in to market on huntin' horses what they'd refuse hundhreds iv pounds for from officers in the Curragh an' the quality. Begor, but some iv thim an' the dhrovers was rare min in a fight. More nor wance I seen them, forty, maybe half a hundred, strong, clear and market-place at Banagher or Athy. Well do I remimber the way the big, red, hairy wrists iv thim'd go up in the air, an' down'd come the springy ground-ash saplins what they carried for switches. The whole lot iv thim wanted to come coortin' the widdy; but sorra wan iv her'd look at thim. She'd flirt an' be coy an' taze thim and make thim mad for love iv her, as weemin likes to do. Thank God for the same! for mayhap we min wouldn't love thim as we do only for their thricky ways; an' thin what'd become iv the counthry wid nothin' in it at all except single min an' ould maids jist dyin', and growin' crabbed for want iv childher to kiss an' tache an' shpank an' make love to? Shure, yer 'ann'rs, 'tis childher as makes the heart iv man green, jist as it is fresh wather than makes the grass grow. Divil a shtep nearer would the widdy iver let mortial man come. "No," she'd say; "whin I see a man fit to fill Mick's place, I'll let yez know iv it; thank ye kindly"; an' wid that she'd shake her head till the beautiful red hair iv it'd be like shparks iv fire— an' the min more mad for her nor iver.

'But, mind ye, she wasn't no shpoil-shport; Mick's wife knew more nor that, an' his widdy didn't forgit the thrick iv it. She'd lade the laugh herself if 'twas anything a dacent woman could shmile at; an' if it wasn't, she'd send the girrls aff to their beds, an' tell the min they might go on talkin' that way, for there was only herself to be insulted; an' that'd shut thim up pretty quick I'm tellin' yez. But av any iv thim'd thry to git affectionate, as min do whin they've had all they can carry, well, thin she had a playful way iv dalin' wid thim what'd always turn the laugh agin' thim. She used to say that she larned the beginnin' iv it at the school an' the rest iv it from Mick. She always kep by her on the counther iv the bar wan iv thim rattan canes wid the curly ends, what the soldiers carries whin they can't borry a whip, an' are goin' out wid their cap on three hairs, an' thim new oiled, to scorch the girrls. An' thin whin any iv the shuitors'd get too affectionate she'd lift the cane an' swish them wid it, her laughin' out iv her like mad all the time. At first wan or two iv the min'd say that a kiss at the widdy was worth a clip iv a cane; an' wan iv thim, a warrm horse-farmer from Poul-a-Phoka, said he'd complate the job av she was to cut him into ribbons. But she was a handy woman wid the cane—which was shtrange enough, for she had no childer to be practisin' on—an' whin she threw what was left iv him back over the bar, wid his face like a gridiron, the other min what was laughin' along wid her tuk the lesson to hearrt. Whinniver afther that she laid her hand on the cane, no matther how quitely, there'd be no more talk iv thryin' for kissin' in that quarther.

'Well, at the time I'm comin' to there was great divarshuns intirely goin' on in the town. The fair was on the morra, an' there was a power iv people in the town; an' cattle, an' geese, an' tur-keys, an' butther, an' pigs, an' vegetables, an' all kinds iv divil-ment, includin' a berryin'—the same bein' an ould attorneyman, savin' yer prisince; a lone man widout friends lyin' out there in the gran' room iv the hotel what they call the "Queen's Room". Well, I needn't tell yer 'ann'rs that the place was pretty full that night. Musha, but it's the fleas themselves what had the bad time iv it, wid thim crowded out on the outside, an' shakin', an' thrim-blin' wid the cowld. The widdy, av coorse, was in the bar passin' the time iv the day wid all that kem in, an' keepin' her eyes afore an' ahint her to hould the girrls up to their wurrk an' not to be thriflin' wid the min. My! but there was a power iv min at the bar that night; warrm farmers from four counties, an' graziers wid their ground-ash plants an' big frieze coats, an' plinty iv commer-cials, too. In the middle iv it all, up the shtreet at a hand gallop comes an Athy carriage wid two horses, an' pulls up at the door wid the horses shmokin'. An' begor', the man in it was smokin' too, a big cygar nigh as long as yer arrm. He jumps out an' walks up as bould as brass to the bar, jist as if there was niver a livin' sowl but himself in the place. He chucks the widdy undher the chin at wanst, an', taking aff his hat, sez:

'"I want the best room in the house. I travel for Shorrox', the greatest long-cotton firrm in the whole worrld, an' I want to open up a new line here! The best is what I want, an' that's not good enough for me!"

'Well, gintlemin, ivery wan in the place was spacheless at his impidence; an', begor! that was the only time in her life I'm tould whin the widdy was tuk back. But, glory be, it didn't take long for her to recover herself, an' sez she quietly:

'"I don't doubt ye, sur! The best can't be too good for a gintle-man what makes himself so aisy at home!" an' she shmiled at him till her teeth shone like jools.

'God knows, gintlemin, what does be in weemin's minds whin they're dalin' wid a man! Maybe it was that Widdy Byrne only wanted to kape the pace wid all thim min crowdin' roun' her, an' thim clutchin' on tight to their shticks an' aiger for a fight wid any man on her account. Or maybe it was that she forgive him his impidence; for well I know that it's not the most modest man, nor him what kapes his distance, that the girrls, much less the widdies, likes the best. But anyhow she spake out iv her to the man from Manchesther:

'"I'm sorry, sur, that I can't give ye the best room—what we call the best—for it is engaged already."

'"Then turn him out!" sez he.

'"I can't," she says—"at laste not till tomorra; an' ye can have the room thin iv ye like."

'There was a kind iv a sort iv a schnicker among some iv the min, thim knowin' iv the corp, an' the Manchesther man tuk it that they was laughin' at him; so he sez:

'"I'll shleep in that room tonight; the other gintleman can put up wid me iv I can wid him. Unless," sez he, oglin' the widdy, "I can have the place iv the masther iv the house, if there's a priest or a parson handy in this town—an' sober," sez he.

'Well, tho' the widdy got as red as a Claddagh cloak, she jist laughed an' turned aside, sayin':

'"Throth, sur, but it's poor Mick's place ye might have, an' welkim, this night."

'"An' where might that be now, ma'am?" sez he, lanin over the bar; an' him would have chucked her under the chin agin, only that she moved her head away that quick.

'"In the churchyard!" she sez. "Ye might take Mick's place there, av ye like, an' I'll not be wan to say ye no."

'At that the min round all laughed, an' the man from Manchesther got mad, an' shpoke out, rough enough too it seemed:

'"Oh, he's all right where he is. I daresay he's quieter times where he is than whin he had my luk out. Him an' the devil can toss for choice in bein' lonely or bein' quite."

'Wid that the widdy blazes up all iv a suddint, like a live sod shtuck in the thatch, an' sez she:

'"Who are ye that dares to shpake ill iv the dead, an' to couple his name wid the divil, an' to his widdy's very face? It's aisy seen that poor Mick is gone!" an' wid that she threw her apron over her head an' sot down an' rocked herself to and fro, as widdies do whin the fit is on thim iv missin' the dead.

'There was more nor wan man there what'd like to have shtud opposite the Manchesther man wid a bit iv a blackthorn in his hand; but they knew the widdy too well to dar to intherfere till they were let. At length wan iv thim—Mr Hogan from nigh Portarlington, a warrm man, that'd put down a thousand pounds iv dhry money any day in the week—kem over to the bar an' tuk aff his hat, an' sez he:

'"Mrs Byrne, ma'am, as a friend of poor dear ould Mick, I'd be glad to take his quarrel on meself on his account, an' more than proud to take it on his widdy's, if, ma'am, ye'll only honour me be saying the wurrd."

'Wid that she tuk down the apron from aff iv her head an' wiped away the tears in her jools iv eyes wid the corner iv it.

'"Thank ye kindly," sez she; "but, gintlemin, Mick an' me run this hotel long together, an' I've run it alone since thin, an' I mane to go on runnin' it be meself, even if new min from Manchesther itself does be bringin' us new ways. As to you, sur," sez she, turnin' to him, "it's powerful afraid I am that there isn't accommodation here for a gintlemin what's so requireful. An' so I think I'll be askin' ye to find convanience in some other hotel in the town."

'Wid that he turned on her an' sez, "I'm here now, an' I offer to pay me charges. Be the law ye can't refuse to resave me or refuse me lodgmint, especially whin I'm on the primises."

'So the Widdy Byrne drewed herself up, an' sez she, "Sur, ye ask yer legal rights; ye shall have them. Tell me what it is ye require."

'Sez he sthraight out: "I want the best room."

'"I've tould you already," sez she, "there's a gintleman in it."

'"Well," sez he, "what other room have ye vacant?"

'"Sorra wan at all,' sez she. "Every room in the house is tuk. Perhaps, sur, ye don't think or remimber that there's a fair on tomorra."

'She shpoke so polite that ivery man in the place knew there

49

was somethin' comin'—later on. The Manchesther man felt that the laugh was on him; but he didn't want for impidence, so he up, an' sez he:

'"Thin, if I have to share wid another, I'll share wid the best! It's the Queen's Room I'll be shleepin' in this night."

'Well, the min shtandin' by wasn't too well plazed wid what was going on; for the man from Manchesther he was plumin' himself for all the worrld like a cock on a dunghill. He laned agin over the bar an' began makin' love to the widdy hot an' fast. He was a fine, shtout-made man, wid a bull neck on to him an' short hair, like wan iv thim "two-to-wan-bar-wans" what I've seen at Punchestown an' Fairy House an' the Galway races. But he seemed to have no manners at all in his coortin', but done it as quick an' business-like as takin' his commercial ordhers. It was like this: "I want to make love; you want to be made love to, bein' a woman. Hould up yer head!"

'We all could see that the widdy was boilin' mad; but, to do him fair, the man from Manchesther didn't seem to care what any wan thought. But we all seen what he didn't see at first, that the widdy began widout thinkin' to handle the rattan cane on the bar. Well, prisintly he began agin to ask about his room, an' what kind iv a man it was that was to share it wid him.

'So sez the widdy, "A man wid less wickedness in him nor you have, an' less impidence."

'"I hope he's a quite man," sez he.

'So the widdy began to laugh, an' sez she: "I'll warrant he's quite enough."

'"Does he shnore? I hate a man—or a woman ayther—what shnores."

'"Throth," sez she, "there's no shnore in him"; an' she laughed agin.

'Some iv the min round what knew iv the ould attorney-man— saving yer prisince—began to laugh too; and this made the Manchesther man suspicious. When the likes iv him gets suspicious he gets rale nasty; so he sez, wid a shneer:

'"You seem to be pretty well up in his habits, ma'am!"

'The widdy looked round at the graziers, what was clutchin' their ash plants hard, an' there was a laughin' divil in her eye that kep' thim quite; an' thin she turned round to the man, and sez she:

50

' "Oh, I know that much, anyhow, wid wan thing an' another, begor!"

'But she looked more enticin' nor iver at that moment. For sure the man from Manchesther thought so, for he laned nigh his whole body over the counther, an' whispered somethin' at her, puttin' out his hand as he did so, an' layin' it on her neck to dhraw her to him. The widdy seemed to know what was comin', an' had her hand on the rattan; so whin he was draggin' her to him an' puttin' out his lips to kiss her—an' her first as red as a turkey-cock an' thin as pale as a sheet—she ups wid the cane and gev him wan skelp across the face wid it, shpringin' back as she done so. Oh jool! but that was a skelp! A big wale iv blood riz up as quick as the blow was shtruck, jist as I've seen on the pigs' backs whin they do be prayin' aloud not to be tuk where they're wanted.

' "Hands off, Misther Impidence!" sez she. The man from Manchesther was that mad that he ups wid the tumbler forninst him an' was goin' to throw it at her, whin there kem an odd sound from the graziers—a sort of "Ach!" as whin a man is workin a sledge, an' I seen the ground-ash plants an' the big fists what held thim, and the big hairy wrists go up in the air. Begor, but polis thimselves wid bayonets wouldn't care to face thim like that! In the half of two twos the man from Manchesther would have been cut in ribbons, but there came a cry from the widdy what made the glasses ring:

' "Shtop! I'm not goin' to have any fightin' here; an' besides, there's bounds to the bad manners iv even a man from Shorrox'. He wouldn't dar to shtrike me—though I have no head! Maybe I hit a thought too hard; but I had rayson to remimber that somethin' was due on Mick's account too. I'm sorry, sur," sez she to the man, quite polite, "that I had to defind meself; but whin a gintleman claims the law to come into a house, an' thin assaults th' owner iv it, though she has no head, it's more restrainful he should be intirely!"

' "Hear, hear!" cried some iv the min, an' wan iv thim sez "Amen," sez he, an' they all begin to laugh. The Manchesther man he didn't know what to do; for begor he didn't like the look of thim ash plants up in the air, an' yit he was not wan to like the laugh agin' him or to take it aisy. So he turns to the widdy an' he lifts his hat an' sez he wid mock politeness:

' "I must complimint ye, ma'am, upon the shtrength iv yer arrm, as upon the mildness iv yer disposition. Throth, an' I'm thinkin' that it's misther Mick that has the best iv it, wid his body lyin' paceful in the churchyard, anyhow; though the poor sowl doesn't seem to have much good in changin' wan devil for another!' An' he looked at her rale spiteful.

'Well, for a minit her eyes blazed, but thin she shmiled at him, an made a low curtsey, an' sez she—oh! mind ye, she was a gran' woman at givin' back as good as she got—

'"Thank ye kindly, sur, for yer polite remarks about me arrm. Sure me poor dear Mick often said the same; only he said more an' wid shuparior knowledge! 'Molly,' sez he—'I'd mislike the shtrength iv yer arrm whin ye shtrike, only that I forgive ye for it whin it comes to the huggin'!' But as to poor Mick's prisint condition I'm not goin' to argue wid ye, though I can't say that I forgive ye for the way you've shpoke iv him that's gone. Bedad, it's fond iv the dead y'are, for ye seem onable to kape thim out iv yer mouth. Maybe ye'll be more respectful to thim before ye die!"

'"I don't want no sarmons!" sez he, wery savage. "Am I to have me room to-night, or am I not?"

'"Did I undherstand ye to say," sez she, "that ye wanted a share iv the Queen's Room?"

'"I did! an' I demand it."

'"Very well, sur," sez she very quietly, "ye shall have it!" Jist thin the supper war ready, and most iv the min at the bar thronged into the coffee-room an among thim the man from Manchesther, what wint bang up to the top iv the table an sot down as though he owned the place, an' him niver in the house before. A few iv the bhoys shtayed a minit to say another word to the widdy, an' as soon as they was alone Misther Hogan up, an' sez he:

'"Oh, darlint! but it's a jool iv a woman y'are! Do ye raly mane to put him in the room wid the corp?"

'"He said he insisted on being in that room!" she says, quite sarious; an' thin givin' a look undher her lashes at the bhoys as made thim lep, sez she:

'"Oh! min, an ye love me give him his shkin that full that he'll tumble into his bed this night wid his sinses obscurified. Dhrink toasts till he misremimbers where he is! Whist! Go, quick, so that he won't suspect nothin'!"

'That was a warrm night, I'm telling ye! The man from Shorrox' had wine galore wid his mate; an' afther, whin the plates an' dishes was tuk away an the nuts was brought in, Hogan got up an' proposed his health, an wished him prosperity in his new line. Iv coorse he had to dhrink that; an' thin others got up, an' there was more toasts dhrunk than there was min in the room, till the man, him not bein' used to whisky punch, began to git onsartin in his shpache. So they gev him more toasts—"Ireland as a nation", an' "Home Rule", an' "The mimory iv Dan O'Connell", an' "Bad luck to Boney", an' "God save the Queen", an' "More power to Manchesther", an' other things what they thought would plaze him, him bein' English. Long hours before it was time for the house to shut, he was as dhrunk as a whole row of fiddlers, an' kep shakin' hands wid ivery man an' promisin' thim to open a new line in Home Rule, an' sich nonsinse. So they tuk him up to the door iv the Queen's Room an' left him there.

'He managed to undhress himself all except his hat, and got into bed wid the corp iv th' ould attorney-man, an' thin an' there fell asleep widout noticin' him.

'Well, prisintly he woke wid a cowld feelin' all over him. He had lit no candle, an' there was only the light from the passage comin' in through the glass over the door. He felt himself nigh fallin' out iv the bed wid him amost on the edge, an' the cowld shtrange gintleman lyin' shlap on the broad iv his back in the middle. He had enough iv the dhrink in him to be quarrelsome.

'"I'll throuble ye,' sez he, "to kape over yer own side iv the bed—or I'll soon let ye know the rayson why." An' wid that he give him a shove. But iv coorse the ould attorney-man tuk no notice whatsumiver.

'"Y'are not that warrm that one'd like to lie contagious to ye," sez he. "Move over, I say, to yer own side!" But divil a shtir iv the corp.

'Well, thin he began to get fightin' angry, an' to kick an' shove the corp; but not gittin' any answer at all at all, he turned round an' hit him a clip on the side iv the head.

'"Git up," he sez, "iv ye're a man at all, an' put up yer dooks."

'Then he got more madder shtill, for the dhrink was shtirrin' in him, an' he kicked an' shoved an' grabbed him be the leg an' the arrm to move him.

'"Begor!" sez he, "but ye're the cowldest chap I iver kem anigh iv. Musha! but yer hairs is like icicles."

'Thin he tuk him be the head, an' shuk him an' brung him to the bedside, an' kicked him clane out on to the flure on the far side iv the bed.

'"Lie there," he sez, "ye ould blast furnace! Ye can warrm yerself up on the flure till to-morra."'

'Be this time the power iv the dhrink he had tuk got ahoult iv him agin, an' he fell back in the middle iv the bed, wid his head on the pilla an' his toes up, an' wint aff ashleep, like a cat in the frost.

'By-an'-by, whin the house was about shuttin' up, the watcher from th' undhertaker's kem to sit be the corp till the mornin', an' th' attorney him bein' a Protestan' there was no candles. Whin the house was quite, wan iv the girrls, what was coortin' wid the watcher, shtole into the room.

'"Are ye there, Michael?" sez she.

'"Yis, me darlint!" he sez, comin' to her; an' there they shtood be the door, wid the lamp in the passage shinin' on the red heads iv the two iv thim.

'"I've come," sez Katty, "to kape ye company for a bit, Michael; for it's crool lonesome worrk sittin' there alone all night. But I mustn't shtay long, for they're all goin' to bed soon, when the dishes is washed up."

'"Give us a kiss," sez Michael.

'"Oh, Michael!" sez she: "kissin' in the prisince iv a corp! It's ashamed iv ye I am."

'"Sorra cause, Katty. Sure, it's more respectful than any other way. Isn't it next to kissin' in the chapel?—an' ye do that whin ye're bein' married. If ye kiss me now, begor but I don't know as it's mortial nigh a weddin' it is! Anyhow, give us a kiss, an' we'll talk iv the rights an' wrongs iv it aftherwards."

"Well, somehow, yer 'ann'rs, that kiss was bein' gave—an' a kiss in the prisince iv a corp is a sarious thing an' takes a long time. Thim two was payin' such attintion to what was going on betune thim that they didn't heed nothin', whin suddint Katty stops, and sez:

'"Whist! what is that?"

'Michael felt creepy too, for there was a quare sound comin' from the bed. So they grabbed one another as they shtud in the doorway an' looked at the bed almost afraid to breathe till the hair on both iv thim began to shtand up in horror; for the corp rose up in the bed, an' they seen it pointin' at thim, an' heard a hoarse voice say—

' "It's in hell I am!—Divils around me! Don't I see thim burnin' wid their heads like flames? an' it's burnin' I am too—burnin', burnin', burnin'! Me throat is on fire, an' me face is burnin'! Wather! wather! Give me wather, if only a dhrop on me tongue's tip!"

'Well, thin Katty let one screetch out iv her, like a wake the dead, an' tore down the passage till she kem to the shtairs, and tuk a flyin' lep down an' fell in a dead faint on the mat below; and Michael yelled 'murdher' wid all his might.

'It wasn't long till there was a crowd in that room, I tell ye; an' a mighty shtrange thing it was that sorra wan iv the graziers had even tuk his coat from aff iv him to go to bed, or laid by his shtick. An' the widdy too, she was as nate an' tidy as iver, though seemin' surprised out iv a sound shleep, an' her clothes onto her, all savin' a white bedgown, an' a candle in her hand. There was some others what had been in bed, min an' wimin wid their bare feet an' slippers on to some iv thim, wid their bracers down their backs, an' their petticoats flung on anyhow. An' some iv thim in big nightcaps, an' some wid their hair all screwed up in knots wid little wisps iv paper, like farden screws iv Limerick twist or Lundy Foot snuff. Musha! but it was the ould weemin what was afraid iv things what didn't alarrm the young wans at all. Divil resave me! but the sole thing they seemed to dhread was the min—dead or alive it was all wan to thim—an' 'twas ghosts an' corpses an' mayhap divils that the rest was afraid iv.

'Well, whin the Manchesther man seen thim all come tumblin into the room he began to git his wits about him; for the dhrink was wearin' aff, an' he was thryin' to remimber where he was. So whin he seen the widdy he put his hand up to his face where the red welt was, an' at wance seemed to undhershtand, for he got mad agin an' roared out:

' "What does this mane? Why this invasion iv me chamber? Clear out the whole kit, or I'll let yez know!" Wid that he was goin' to jump out of bed, but the moment they seen his toes the ould weemin let a screech out iv thim, an' clung to the min an' implored thim to save thim from murdher—an' worse. An' there was the Widdy Byrne laughin' like mad; an' Misther Hogan shtepped out, an' sez he:

'"Do jump out, Misther Shorrox! The boys has their switches, an' it's a mighty handy costume ye're in for a leatherin'!"

'So wid that he jumped back into bed an' covered the clothes over him.

'"In the name of God," sez he, "what does it all mane?"

'"It manes this," sez Hogan, goin' round the bed an' draggin' up the corp an' layin' it on the bed beside him. "Begorra! but it's a cantankerous kind iv a scut y'are. First nothin' will do ye but sharin' a room wid a corp: an' thin ye want the whole place to yerself.'

'"Take it away! Take it away," he yells out.

'"Begorra," sez Mister Hogan, "I'll do no such thing. The gintleman ordhered the room first, an' it's he has the right to ordher you to be brung out!"

'"Did he shnore much, sur?" says the widdy; an' wid that she burst out laughin' an' cryin' all at wanst. "That'll tache ye to shpake ill iv the dead agin!" An' she flung her petticoat over her head an run out iv the room.

'Well, we turned the min all back to their own rooms; for the most part iv thim had plenty iv dhrink on board, an' we feared for a row. Now that the fun was over, we didn't want any unplisintness to follow. So two iv the graziers wint into wan bed, an' we put the man from Manchesther in th' other room, an' gev him a screechin' tumbler iv punch to put the hearrt in him agin.

'I thought the widdy had gone to her bed; but whin I wint to put out the lights I seen one in the little room behind the bar, an' I shtepped quite, not to dishturb her, and peeped in. There she was on a low shtool rockin' herself to an' fro, an' goin' on wid her laughin' an' cryin' both together, while she tapped wid her fut on the flure. She was talkin' to herself in a kind iv a whisper, an' I heerd her say:

'"Oh, but its the crool woman I am to have such a thing done in me house—an' that poor sowl, wid none to weep for him, knocked about that a way for shport iv dhrunken min—while me poor dear darlin' himself is in the cowld clay!—But oh! Mick, Mick, if ye were only here! Wouldn't it be you—you wid the fun iv ye an' yer merry hearrt—that'd be plazed wid the doin's iv this night!"'

A HOUSE POSSESSED

Sax Rohmer

I strode briskly up the long beech avenue. The snow that later was to carpet the drive and to clothe the limbs of the great trees, now hung suspended in dull grey cloud banks over Devrers Hall. This I first set eyes upon the place.

Earl Ryland had seen it from the car when motoring to Stratford, had delayed one hour and twenty-five minutes to secure the keys and look over the house, and had leased it for three years. That had been two days ago. Now, as I passed the rusty, iron gates and walked up the broad stairs of the terrace to the front door, the clatter of buckets and a swish of brushes told me that the workmen were busy within. It is, after all, a privilege to be the son of a Wall Street hustler.

Faithful to my promise, I inspected the progress made by the decorating contractor, and proceeded to look over the magnificent old mansion. Principally, I believe, it was from designs by Vanbrugh. The banqueting hall impressed me particularly with its fretwork ceiling, elaborate mouldings, and its large, stone-mullioned windows with many-hued, quarrel-pane lattices.

I had this wing of the building quite to myself, and passing through into what may have been a library, I saw at the farther end a low, arched door in the wall. It was open, and a dim light showed beyond. I approached it, passed down six stone steps and found myself in a small room, evidently of much earlier date than the rest of the house.

It had an elaborately carved chimney piece reaching to the ceiling, and the panelling was covered with extraordinary designs. One small window lighted the room. Before the window, his back towards me, stood a cowled monk!

At my gasp of mingled fear and surprise, he turned a red, bearded face to me. To my great amazement, I saw that the mysterious intruder was smoking a well coloured briar!

'Did I frighten you?' he inquired, with a strong Irish brogue. 'I'm sorry! But it's years since I saw over Devrers, and so I ventured to trespass. I'm Father Bernard from the monastery yonder. Are you Mr Ryland?'

I gasped again, but with relief. Father Bernard, broad-shouldered and substantial, puffing away at his briar, was no phantom after all, but a very genial mortal.

'No,' I replied. 'He will be down later. I am known as Cumberly.'

He shook my hand very heartily; he seemed on the point of speaking again, yet hesitated.

'What a grand old place it is,' I continued. 'This room surely, is older than the rest?'

'It is part of the older mansion,' he replied, 'Devereaux Hall. Devrers is a corruption.'

'Devereaux Hall,' I said. 'Did it belong to that family?'

Father Bernard nodded.

'Robert Devereaux, Earl of Essex, owned it. There's his crest over the door. He never lived here himself, but if you can make out medieval Latin, this inscription here will tell you who did.'

He watched me curiously while I struggled with the crabbed characters.

'Here by grace of his noble patron, Robert Devereaux, my lord of Essex,' I read, 'laboured Maccabees Nosta of Padua, a pupil of Michel de Notredame, seeking the light.'

'Nosta was a Jewish astrologer and magician,' explained the monk, 'and according to his own account, as you see, a pupil of the notorious Michel de Notredame, or Nostradamus. He lived here under the patronage of the Earl until 1601, when Essex was executed. Legend says that he was not the pupil of Nostradamus, but his master the devil, and that he brought about the fall of his patron. What became of Nosta of Padua nobody knows.'

He paused, watching me with something furtive in his blue eyes.

'I'm a regular guidebook, you're thinking?' he went on. 'Well, so I am. We have it all in the old records at the monastery. A Spanish family acquired the place after the death of Robert Devereaux—the Miguels, they called themselves. They were shunned by the whole country, and it's recorded that they held Black Masses and Devil's Sabbaths here in this very room!'

'Good heavens!' I cried, 'the house has an unpleasant history!'

'The last of them was burned for witchcraft in the market-place at Ashby, as late as 1640!'

I suppose I looked as uncomfortable as I felt, glancing apprehensively about the gloomy apartment.

'When Devereaux or Devrers Hall was pulled down and rebuilt, this part was spared for some mysterious reason. But let me tell you that from 1640 till 1863—when a Mr Nicholson leased it—nobody has been able to live here!'

'What do you mean? Ghosts?'

'No, fires!'

'Fires!'

'That same! If you'll examine the rooms closely, you'll find that some of them have been rebuilt and some partially rebuilt, at dates long after Vanbrugh's day. It's where the fires have been! Seven poor souls have burned to death in Devrers since the Miguels' time, but the fires never spread beyond the rooms they broke out in!'

'Father Bernard,' I said, 'tell me no more at present! This is horrible! Some of the best friends I have are coming to spend Christmas here!'

'I'd have warned Mr Ryland if he'd given me time,' continued the monk. 'But it's likely he'd have laughed at me for my pains! All you can do now, Mr Cumberly, is to say nothing about it until after Christmas. Then induce him to leave. I'm not a narrow-minded man, and I'm not a superstitious one, I think, but if facts are facts, Devrers Hall is *possessed*!'

The party that came together that Christmas at Devrers Hall was quite the most ideal that one could have wished for or imagined. There was no smart set boredom, for Earl's friends were not smart set bores. Old and young there were, and children too. What Christmas gathering is complete without children?

Mr Ryland, Sr, and Mrs Ryland were over from New York, and the hard-headed man of affairs proved the most charming old gentleman one could have desired at a Christmas party. A Harvard friend of Earl's, the Rev. Lister Hanson, Mrs Hanson, Earl's sister, and two young Hansons were there. They, with Mrs Van Eyck, a pretty woman of thirty whose husband was never seen in her company, completed the American contingent.

But Earl had no lack of English friends, and these, to the round number of twenty, assisted at the Christmas house-warming.

On the evening of the twenty-third of December, as I entered the old banqueting hall bright with a thousand candles, the warm light from the flaming logs danced upon the oak leaves, emblems of hospitality which ornamented the frieze. Searching out strange heraldic devices upon the time-blackened panelling, I stood in the open door in real admiration.

A huge Christmas tree occupied one corner by the musicians' gallery, and around this a group of youngsters had congregated, looking up in keen anticipation at the novel gifts which swung from the frosted branches. My Ryland, Sr, his wife and another grey-haired lady, with Father Bernard from the monastery, sat upon the black oak settles by the fire; they were an oddly assorted, but merry group. In short, the interior of the old hall made up a picture that would have delighted the soul of Charles Dickens.

'It's just perfect, Earl!' came Hanson's voice.

I turned, and saw that he and Earl Ryland stood at my elbow.

'It will be, when Mona comes!' was the reply.

'What has delayed Miss Verek?' I asked. Earl's fiancée, Mona Verek, and her mother were to have joined us that afternoon.

'I can't quite make out from her wire,' he answered quietly, a puzzled frown ruffing his forehead. 'But she will be here by tomorrow, Christmas Eve.'

Hanson clapped him on the back and smiled. 'Bear up, Earl,' he said. 'Hello! here comes Father Bernard, and he's been yarning again. Just look how your governor is laughing.'

Earl turned, as with a bold gait the priest came towards them, his face radiating with smiles, his eyes alight with amusement. It was certainly a hilarious group the monk had left behind him. As he joined us, he linked his arm in that of the American clergyman and drew him aside for a private chat, I thought what a broad-minded company we were. When the two, in intimate conversation, walked off together, they formed one of the most pleasant pictures imaginable. The true spirit of Christmas reigned.

I passed to an oak settee where Justin Grinley, his wife and small daughter were pulling crackers with Mrs Hanson, just as young Lawrence Bowman appeared from a side door.

'Have you seen Mrs Van Eyck?' he inquired quickly.

No one had seen her for some time, and young Bowman hurried off upon his quest.

Grinley raised quizzical eyebrows, but said nothing. In point of fact, Bowman's attentions to the lady had already excited some comment; but Mrs Van Eyck was an old friend of the Rylands, and we relied upon her discretion to find a nice girl among the company—there were many—to take the romantic youth off her hands.

Father Bernard presently beckoned to me from the door beneath the musicians' gallery.

'You have, of course, said nothing of the matters we know of?' he asked, as I joined him.

I shook my head, and the monk smiled around on the gathering.

'The old sorcerer's study is fitted up as a cozy corner, I see,' he continued, 'but between ourselves, I shouldn't let any of the young people stay long in there!' He met my eyes seriously.

'If, indeed, the enemy holds power within Devrers, I think there is no likely victim among you tonight. The legend of Devrers Hall, you must know, Mr Cumberly, is that Maccabees Nosta, or the arch enemy in person, appears here in response to the slightest evil thought, word or deed within the walls! If any company could hope to exclude him, it is the present!' This he said half humorously and with his eyes roaming again over the merry groups about the great lighted room. 'But, please God, the evil has passed.'

He was about to take his leave, for he came and went at will, a privileged visitor, as others of the Brotherhood. I walked with him along the gallery, lined now with pictures from Earl Ryland's collection. One of the mullioned windows was open.

Out of the darkness we looked for a moment over the dazzling white carpet which lay upon the lawn, to where a fairy shrubbery, backed by magical, white trees, glittered as though diamond-dusted under the frosty moon. A murmur of voices came, and two figures passed across the snow: a woman in a dull red cloak with a furred collar and a man with a heavy travelling coat worn over his dress clothes. His arm was about the woman's waist.

The monk made no sign, leaving me at the gallery door with a deep 'Good night.'

But I saw his cowled figure silhouetted against a distant window, and his hand was raised in the ancient form of benediction.

Alone in the long gallery, something of the gaiety left me. By the open window, I stood for a moment looking out, but no one was visible now. The indiscreet dalliance of Mrs Van Eyck with a lad newly down from Cambridge seemed so utterly out of the picture. The lawn on that side of the house was secluded, but I knew that Father Bernard had seen and recognised them. I knew, too, the thought that was in his mind. As I passed slowly back towards the banqueting hall, my footsteps striking hollowly upon the oaken floor, that thought grew in significance. Free as I was, or as I thought I was, from the medieval superstitions which possibly were part of the monk's creed, I shuddered at remembrance of the unnamable tragedies which this gallery might have staged.

It was very quiet. As I came abreast of the last window, the moonlight through a stained quarrel pane spread a red patch across the oaken floor, and I passed it quickly. It had almost the look of a fire burning beneath the woodwork!

Then, through the frosty, night air, I distinctly heard the great bell tolling out, from up the beech avenue at the lodge gate.

I was anxious to know what it meant myself. But Earl, whose every hope and every fear centred in Mona Verek, outran me easily. I came up to the lodge gates just as he threw them open in his madly impulsive way. The lodge was unoccupied, for the staff was incomplete, and a servant had fastened the gates for the night after Father Bernard had left.

The monk could not have been gone two minutes, but now in the gateway stood a tall man enveloped in furs, who rested one hand upon the shoulder of a chauffeur. It had begun to snow again.

'What's the matter?' cried Ryland anxiously, as the man who attended to the gates tardily appeared. 'Accident?'

The stranger waved his disengaged hand with a curiously foreign gesture, and showed his teeth in a smile. He had a black, pointed beard and small moustache, with fine, clear-cut features and commanding eyes.

'Nothing serious,' he replied. Something in his voice reminded me of a note in a great organ, it was so grandly deep and musical. 'My man was blinded by a drive of snow and ran us off the road. I fear my ankle is twisted, and the car being temporarily disabled . . .'

With the next house nearly two miles away, that was explanation enough for Earl Ryland. Very shortly we were assisting the distinguished-looking stranger along the avenue, Earl pooh-poohing his protests and sending a man ahead to see that a room would be ready. The snow was falling now in clouds, and Ryland and I were covered. At the foot of the terrace stairs, with cheery light streaming out through the snowladen air, I noted something that struck me as odd, but at the time as no more than that.

Not a flake of snow rested upon the stranger, from the crown of his black fur cap to the edge of his black fur coat!

Before I had leisure to consider this circumstance, which a moment's thought must have shown to be a curious phenomenon, our unexpected visitor spoke.

'I have a slight face wound, occasioned by broken glass,' he said. For the first time, I saw that it was so. 'I would not alarm your guests unnecessarily. Could we enter by a more private door?'

'Certainly!' cried Ryland heartily. 'This way, sir.'

So, unseen by the rest of the party, we entered by the door in the tower of the south wing and lodged the stranger in one of the many bedrooms there. He was profuse in his thanks, but declined any medical aid other than that of his saturnine man. When the blizzard had somewhat abated, he said, the man could proceed to the wrecked car and possibly repair it well enough to enable them to continue their journey. He would trespass upon our good nature no longer; an hour's rest was all that he required.

'You must not think of leaving tonight,' said Ryland cordially. 'I will see that your wants are attended to.'

His man entered, carrying a bag; we left him descending again to the hall.

'Why!' cried Earl, 'I never asked him his name and never told him mine!'

He laughed at his own absentmindedness, and we rejoined his guests. But an indefinable change had come over the party. The blizzard was increasing in violence, so that now it shrieked around Devrers Hall like a regiment of ghouls. The youthful members, numbering five, had been sent off to bed, and into the hearts of the elders of the company had crept a general predilection for the fireside. Our entrance created quite a sensation.

'Why,' cried Ryland, 'I believe you took us for bogeys. Who's been telling ghost stories?'

Mrs Van Eyck stretched a dainty foot to the blaze and writhed her white shoulders expressively.

'Mr Hanson has been talking about the Salem witch trials,' she said, turning her eyes to Earl. 'I don't know why he likes to frighten us!'

'There was an alleged witch burned at Ashby, near here, as recently as 1640,' continued Hanson. 'I remember reading about it in a work on the subject; a young Spanish woman, of great beauty, too, called Isabella de Miguel, I believe.'

I started. The conversation was turning in a dangerous direction. Old Mr Ryland laughed, but not mirthfully.

'Quit demons and witches,' he said. 'Let's find a more humorous topic, not that I stand for such nonsense.'

Three crashing blows, sounding like those of a titanic hammer on an anvil, rang through the house. An instant's silence followed, then a frightened chorus: 'What was that?'

No one could imagine, and Earl had been as startled as the rest of us. He ran from the room, and I followed him. The wind howled and whistled with ever increasing violence. At the low arched door leading to the domestic offices, we found a group of panic-stricken servants huddled together.

'What was that noise?' asked Earl sharply.

His American butler, Knowlson, who formed one of the group, came forward. 'It seemed to come from upstairs, sir,' he said. 'But I don't know what can have caused it.'

'Come and look, then.'

Up the massive staircase we went, Knowlson considerably in the rear. But though we searched everywhere assiduously, there was nothing to show what had occasioned the noise. Leaving Ryland peeping in at his two small nephews, who proved to be slumbering peacefully, I went up three steps and through a low archway, and found myself in the south wing. The only occupant, as far as I knew, was the injured stranger. A bright light shone

under his door, and I wondered how many candles he had burning.
I knocked.

A gust of wind shrieked furiously around the building, then subsided to a sound like the flapping of wings.

The door was opened a few inches. The light almost dazzled me. I had a glimpse of the unbidden guest, and saw that he wore a loose dressing gown of an unusual shade of red.

'Has anything disturbed you?' I asked.

'No,' he replied, with much concern in his deep, organ voice, yet his black eyes were laughing. 'Why do you ask?'

'We heard a strange noise,' I answered shortly. 'Is your ankle better?'

'I thank you—very much,' he said, 'I am awaiting my man's report respecting the state of the car.'

There was nothing in his handsome dark face, in his deep voice, or even in his laughing eyes to justify it, but at that moment I felt certain, beyond any possibility of doubt, that the noise had come from his room. I wanted to run! In fact, I do not know how I might have acted, if Ryland hadn't joined me.

'Sorry to have disturbed you,' came his jovial tones, 'but the house is full of funny noises! By the way, I forgot to mention that my name is Wilbur Earl Ryland, and I hope you'll stay just as long as it suits you!'

'I thank you,' was the unemotional reply. 'You are more than kind. I am Count de Stano of Padua. Good night.'

He closed the door.

Again came the wind, shrieking around the end of the wing like a troop of furies; and again came an uncanny flapping. Earl caught at my arm.

'What is it?'

'Did you hear—someone laughing?'

'No,' I said unsteadily. 'It was the howling of the blizzard.'

At the landing, he turned to me again.

'What had the Count burning in his room?' he muttered. 'That wasn't candlelight!'

We found a crowd awaiting us at the foot of the staircase. No one was anxious to go to bed, and arrangements were made by several of the more nervous to share rooms.

'Has the Count's chauffeur returned?' Earl asked Knowlson.

'He's just come into the servants' hall now, sir. He—'

'Lock up, then.'

'He'd been out in all that snow, sir . . .'

'Well?'

'There wasn't a sign of any on his coat.'

The man's voice shook and he glanced back at the group of servants, none of whom seemed disposed to return to their quarters.

'He wore another over it, ass!' snapped Ryland. 'Set about your business, all of you! You are like a pack of children.'

We experienced no further alarms, save from the uncanny howling of the wind, but there were no more ghost stories. Those who went to bed ascended the great oak staircase in parties. Mr Ryland, Earl and I were the last to go, and we parted at last without reference to the matter, of which, I doubt not, all of us were thinking.

Sleep was almost impossible. My quaint little oak-panelled room seemed to rock in a tempest which now had assumed extraordinary violence. For hours I lay listening for that other sound which was not the voice of the blizzard and which, although I had belittled, I had heard as clearly as Earl had heard it.

I detected it at last, just once—a wild, demoniacal laugh.

I leaped to the floor. The sound had not been within the house, I thought, but outside. Clenching my teeth in anticipation of the icy gust which would sweep into the room, I slightly opened the heavily leaded window. The south wing was clearly visible.

Out from the small, square window of the study of Maccabees Nosta poured a beam of fiery light, staining the snow flakes as they swirled madly through its redness.

A moment it shone, and was gone.

I pulled the window fast.

Strange needs teach us strange truths. I was sure in that hour that the simple faith of Father Bernard was greater than all our wisdom, and I would have given much for his company.

For me the pleasures and entertainments of the ensuing day were but gnawing anxieties and fruitless vigils. Who was the man calling himself de Stano? *Stano* was merely a play on *Nosta*. To what place had his chauffeur taken his car to be repaired? Why did he avoid Father Bernard, as that morning I had seen him do? De Stano claimed acquaintance with mutual friends, all of them absent. Earl was too hospitable. A man who could walk, even with the aid of a big ebony stick, could reach the station in a borrowed car and proceed on his journey.

Devrers Hall was nearly empty, but by one pretext or another I had avoided joining any of the parties. As I stood smoking on the terrace, Mrs Van Eyck came out, dressed in a walking habit which displayed her lithe figure almost orientally.

'Mr Bowman and I are walking over to the monastery. Won't you join us, Mr Cumberly?' she said.

'Thank you, but some unexpected work has come to hand and I fear I must decline! Have you seen our new guest recently?'

'The Count? Yes, just a while ago. What a strange man! Do you know, Mr Cumberly, he almost frightens me.'

'Indeed!'

'He is a most accomplished hypnotist! Oh, I must show you! He was angry with me for being sceptical, you know, and suddenly challenged me to touch him, even with my little finger. I did, look!'

She had pulled off her glove and held out her hand. The top of one finger was blistered, as by contact with fire!

'Hypnotic suggestion, of course,' she said laughingly. 'He is not always red hot.'

She laughed gaily as young Bowman came out; the two walking off together.

I re-entered the house.

None of the servants had seen the Count, and when I knocked at his door there was no reply. Passing back along the corridor I met Lister Hanson.

'Hello!' I said. 'I thought you were out with the others.'

'No. I had some trivial matters to attend to; Majorie and the youngsters have gone skating.'

I hesitated.

'Is Earl with them?'

Hanson laughed.

'He has motored over to the station. Mona Verek is due some time within the next three hours.'

Should I confide in him? Yes, I decided, for I could contain my uncanny suspicions no longer.

'What is your opinion of this de Stano?' I asked abruptly.

Hanson's face clouded.

'Curiously enough, I have not met him,' he replied. 'He patently avoids me. In fact, Cumberly, very few of the folks *have* met him. You must have noticed that on one pretence or another he has avoided being present at meals? Though he is living under the same roof, I assure you the bulk of us *have never seen him.*'

It was sufficient. I at any rate felt assured of a hearing, and, drawing Hanson into my own room, I unfolded to him the incredible suspicions which I dared to harbour and which were shared by Father Bernard.

At the end of my story, the young clergyman sat looking out the window. When he turned his face to me, it was unusually serious.

'It is going back to the Middle Ages,' he said, 'but there is nothing in your story that a Churchman may not believe. I have studied the dark pages of history which deal with witchcraft, demonology and possession. I have seen in Germany the testimonies of men as wise as any we have today. Although I can see your expected incredulity and scepticism, I assure you I am at one with Father Bernard upon this matter. The Count de Stano, whoever or whatever he is, must quit this house.'

'But what weapons have we against—'

'Cumberly, if some awful thing in the shape of man is among us, that thing has come in obedience to a summons. Do you know the legend of Devrers Hall, the dreadful history of the place?'

I nodded, greatly surprised.

'You wonder where I learned it? You forget that I have dipped deeply into these matters. Directly after the party broke up, I had intended to induce Earl to leave. Cumberly, the place is unclean.'

'Is there no way of ridding it of—'

'Only by defeating the thing which legend says first appeared here as Maccabees Nosta. And which of us, being human, can hope to brave that ordeal?'

I was silent for some time.

'We must remember, Hanson,' I said, 'that, regarding certain undoubtedly weird happenings in the light of what we know of Devrers, we may have deceived ourselves.'

'We may,' he agreed. 'But we dare not rest until we know that we *have.*'

So together we searched the house for Count de Stano, but failed to meet with him. The storm of the previous night had subsided, and dusk came creeping upon a winter landscape which spoke only of great peace. The guests began to return, in parties, and presently Earl Ryland arrived, looking very worried.

'Mona's missed her train,' he said. 'There seems to be a fatality about the thing.'

Hanson said nothing at the time, but when Earl had gone upstairs to dress, he turned to me.

'You know Mona Verek, of course?'

'Quite well.'

'She justifies all his adoration, Cumberly. She is the nearest thing to an angel that a human can be. I agree with Earl that there is a fatality in her delay! He is going off again after dinner. You know how dreadfully impulsive he is, and I have always at the back of my brain the idea that we may be deluding ourselves.'

It was close to the dinner hour now, and I hurried to my room to dress. The quaint little window, as I already have mentioned, commanded a view of the south wing, and as I stooped to the oaken window seat, groping for the candles, my gaze strayed across the snow-carpeted lawns to where the shrubbery loomed greyly in the growing December dusk.

Two figures passed hurriedly in by the south entrance, Lawrence Bowman and Marie Van Eyck. They would have quick work to dress. I found the candles, then dropped them and stood peering from the window with a horror upon me greater than any I yet had known in that house.

A few paces behind the pair, footsteps were forming in the snow—the footsteps of one invisible, who followed, who came to the southern door and who entered after them. Faint wreaths as of steam floated over the ghostly trail.

'My God!' I whispered. 'My God!'

How I dressed, Heaven only knows. I have no recollection of anything until, finding myself at the foot of the great staircase, I said to Knowlson, struggling to make my voice sound normal, 'Is the Count de Stano in?'

'I think not, sir. I believe he is leaving this evening. But I have never seen the Count personally, sir.'

Looking in at the door of the long apartment which Earl had had converted into a billiard room, I found Bowman adjusting his tie before a small mirror.

'Have you seen the Count?' I asked shortly.

'Yes. He is talking to Marie—to Mrs Van Eyck—in the lounge.'

I set off briskly. There was but one door to the old study, now the lounge. I hoped (and feared, I confess) to meet the Count there face to face.

The place was only lighted by the crackling wood fire on the great hearth and Mrs Van Eyck alone stood leaning against the mantelpiece, the red gleam of the fire upon her bare shoulders.

'I had hoped to find the Count here,' I said, as she turned to me.

'Surely you passed him? He couldn't have reached farther than the library as you came in.'

I shook my head, and for a moment Mrs Van Eyck looked almost afraid.

'Are you sure?' she asked. 'I can't understand it. He is leaving almost immediately, too.'

Her hands were toying with a curious little ornament suspended by a chain about her neck. She saw me looking at it and held it up for my inspection.

'Isn't it odd?' she laughed rather uneasily. 'The Count tells me that it is an ancient Assyrian love charm.'

It was a tiny golden calf, and, unaccountably, I knew that I paled as I looked at it.

The gong sounded.

I met Lister Hanson at the door of the banqueting hall. His quest had proved as futile as mine.

We were a very merry dinner party. Again it seemed impossible to credit the idea that malign powers were at work in our midst. Earl Ryland made himself the object of much good-humoured jest by constantly glancing at his watch.

'I know it's rude,' he said, 'but you don't know how anxious I am about Mona.'

When at last dinner was over, he left the old people to do the honours and rushed away in his impetuous, schoolboy fashion to the waiting car, and so off to the station.

Hanson touched me on the shoulder.

'To the Count's room first,' he whispered.

We slipped away unnoticed and mounted the staircase. On the landing we met Mrs Van Eyck's maid carrying an armful of dresses.

71

'Are you packing?' rapped Hanson, with a sudden suspicion in his voice.

'Yes, sir,' replied the girl. 'My lady has had a message and must leave tonight.'

'Have you seen the Count de Stano?'

'A tall, dark gentleman, carrying a black stick? He has just gone along the passage, sir.'

Hanson stood looking after the maid for a moment.

'I have heard of no messenger,' he said, 'and Van Eyck is due on Christmas morning.'

Along the oak-lined passage and up into the south wing we went. The Count's room was empty. There was no fire in the hearth, but the heat of the place was insupportable, although the window was open.

Something prompted me to glance out. From the edge of the lawn below, across to the frosted shrubbery, extended a track of footprints.

'Look, Hanson!' I said and grasped his arm. 'Look! and tell me if I dream!'

A faint vapour was rising from the prints.

'Let's get our coats and see where they lead,' he said quietly.

It was with an indescribable sense of relief that I quitted the room which the Count de Stano had occupied. We got our coats and prepared to go out. With a suddenness which was appalling, the wind rose and, breaking in upon the frozen calm of the evening, shrieked about Devrers Hall with all the fury of a high gale. With it came snow.

Through that raging blizzard, we fought our way around the angle of the house, leaving the company preparing for the dance in the banqueting hall.

Not a track was to be seen, and the snow was falling in swirling clouds.

We performed a complete circuit of the hall, and in the huge yard we found lamps and lanterns burning. Lawrence Bowman's man was preparing his car for the road; he was driving Mrs Van Eyck to the station, the man said. But both Hanson and I quickly noted that young Bowman's luggage was strapped in place.

Retracing our steps, we saw two snow-covered figures ahead of us, a woman in a dull-red cloak and a man in a big motor coat. They passed on to the terrace, and into the light streaming from the open doors. Earl Ryland had returned. His big Panhard stood at the steps.

'My God! Look!' gasped Hanson, and dragged me back.

I knew what to expect, yet at sight of it my heart stood still.

Steaming footprints appeared, hard upon those of Mrs Van Eyck and Bowman. They pursued a supernatural course on the terrace steps, stopped, and passed away around the north angle of the hall.

'May Heaven protect all here tonight!' prayed the clergyman fervently. 'Follow, follow, Cumberly? At all costs we must follow!' he continued hoarsely.

Which of us trembled the more violently, I do not know. Passing the cheery light of the open doors, we traced the devilish tracks before us. The wind had dropped as suddenly as it had arisen, but snow still fell lightly. Then, from the angle of the great house, we saw a sight which robbed us of what little courage we retained.

Glaring in at the window of the room known as the lantern room, with the light of a great log fire and many candles playing fully upon its malignant face, crouched a red-robed figure. A demon of the Dark Ages it seemed, that clutched and mewed and muttered as it glared. It crouched lower, and lower, then drew back and held its arms before its awful face, thrusting away from it that which approached the window from within. It turned and fled with a shriek unlike anything human or animal, and was gone, leaving behind it steaming footprints in the snow.

A slim shape showed darkly behind the lattice, and the cold light reflected from the snow touched the pure, oval face of Mona Verek.

We fought our way back to the terrace.

'The curse of Devrers Hall in its true form,' muttered Hanson, 'in the red robe of Maccabees Nosta, the Uniform of Satan!'

We could not and dared not, speak of what we had seen, but the gaieties of the night left us cold. As the hours passed and still nothing occurred to break the serenity of the happy gathering, my forebodings grew keener.

Yet, whenever I looked at Mona Verek, fair and fragile, with wonderful blue eyes—which often made me fear that already she was more than half a creature of another sphere—I found new courage.

It was Hanson who first noticed that Mrs Van Eyck and Bowman were missing.

He drew my attention to it at the instant when the tempest, for a while quiescent, awoke to renewed fury.

'Did you hear that?' he whispered.

I saw Earl glance up quickly from an intimate chat with Mona.

Mingled with the song of the storm had arisen fiendish laughter again and the sound of dull flapping. It seemed like the signal for what was to befall.

Knowlson, ghastly white, rushed into the hall.

'Mr Ryland! Mr Ryland!' he cried unceremoniously.

In an instant we were all flocking about the door. Bowman's man, trembling, stood outside.

'I don't know what's become of him, sir,' he said tremulously. 'He and Mrs Van Eyck were to have started at eleven-thirty, and, going in to look for him in the lounge—Oh, my God, sir!—I saw something like a great owl go in at the window.'

We delayed no longer. Out into the blizzard we poured and over the snow to the south wing.

Blue, spirituous flames were belching from the window of the astrologer's study! One shrill scream reached our ears, to be drowned by the mighty voices of the wind.

'Impossible to get in the window,' cried Ryland. 'Around through the library. Form up a line to pass buckets, Knowlson!'

As we rushed up the snow-carpeted terrace steps, Hanson fell. Someone stayed to attend to him. Ryland and I ran on through the house and entered the library together. It was in darkness, but the ancient, iron-studded door leading down into the study was outlined in blue light.

I leapt forward in the gloom, my hand outstretched, and something interposed between me and the door—something fiery. With a muffled yell, I drew back.

Ryland passed me. His form vaguely silhouetted against that weird glow, I saw him raise his arms as if to shield his face. An evidently irresistible force hurled him back, and he fell with a crash at the feet of those who crowded the entrance to the library.

'Oh! my God!' he groaned, struggling to his feet. '*What* is before that door?'

A sound like the roaring of a furnace came from within, with a dull beating on the oak. We stood there in the dark, watching the door. Someone pushed to the front of the group.

'Keep back, Masters,' said Ryland huskily. 'My arms are burned to the elbows. Some hellish thing stands before that door. Keep back, man, till we get lights. Bring lights! Bring lights!'

At that we withdrew from the dark library, until we all stood outside in the hall. Some of us muttered what prayers we knew, while the furnace roared inside and the storm shrieked outside.

There have been some with whom I have discussed these events, who were convinced that these were the result of hallucination combined with the unsuspected presence of an accomplished illusionist and remorseless jester, but I am convinced otherwise.

Mona Verek approached from the direction of the banqueting hall, two trembling servants following with lights. She was very pale, but quite composed.

'Mona!' began Earl huskily, 'there's devil's work! This is no place—'

She stopped him with a quiet little gesture, and took a lamp from one of the men.

'Mr Hanson has explained to me, Earl,' she said. 'He is disabled, or he would be here. I quite understand that there is nothing in the library that can harm me. It can only harm those who fear it. I will unlock the door, Earl, I have promised.'

'Mona! Hanson has asked *you*—'

'You don't understand. He has asked me, because for me there is no danger.'

He would have stopped her, but he forgot his injured arms, and was too late. She went in, believing she would be protected.

Protected she was.

No invisible flame seared her, nothing contested her coming. Entering behind her, he saw her stoop and unlock the door. A cloud of oily, blue-black smoke belched out.

We had thought to find those within past aid, but up the steps Lawrence Bowman staggered, dragging the insensible form of Marie Van Eyck.

'Thank God!' said old Mr Ryland devoutly.

There was a piercing, frenzied shriek. All heard it with horror. One of the Library windows banged open, and a cloud of snow poured into the room.

'There's someone getting out,' cried a man's voice.

'De Stano!' yelled Earl.

Several of us leaped to the window. In the stormy darkness, a red something was racing over the snow towards the beech avenue. The wind dropped, and from the monastery a bell rang.

'The midnight service,' I said.

At the first stroke the red figure stopped dead, turned, and seemed to throw up its arms. It was at that moment, I was told by those near the door, that the strange flames died away in the ancient study, leaving only some charred woodwork to show where the fire had been. The blizzard howled again madly. I was not the only one there who heard amid its howling the sound as of flapping wings.

Mona Verek and Bowman were bending over the insensible woman. Upon her flesh was burned a clear impression of a calf, but the little image itself was missing.

The wind died away, no more snow fell and suddenly, as if a curtain had been raised from before it, the moon sailed into the skies. Marie Van Eyck opened her eyes and looked about her with an expression I shall never forget.

'The fire!' she whispered, 'the fire! What is it?'

The bell ceased tolling.

'It is Christmas morning!' said Mona Verek.

THE MIRACULOUS REVENGE

George Bernard Shaw

                    *   *   *

I arrived in Dublin on the evening of the 5th of August, and drove
to the residence of my uncle, the Cardinal Archbishop. He is, like
most of my family, deficient in feeling, and consequently cold to
me personally. He lives in a dingy house, with a side-long view of
the portico of his cathedral from the front windows, and of a
monster national school from the back. My uncle maintains no
retinue. The people believe that he is waited upon by angels.
When I knocked at the door, an old woman, his only servant,
opened it, and informed me that her master was then officiating
in the cathedral, and that he had directed her to prepare dinner
for me in his absence. An unpleasant smell of salt fish made me
ask her what the dinner consisted of. She assured me that she had
cooked all that could be permitted in His Holiness's house on a
Friday. On my asking her further why on a Friday, she replied
that Friday was a fast day. I bade her tell His Holiness that I had
hoped to have the pleasure of calling on him shortly, and drove
to a hotel in Sackville Street, where I engaged apartments and
dined.

After dinner I resumed my eternal search—I know not for what:
it drives me to and fro like another Cain. I sought in the streets
without success. I went to the theatre. The music was execrable,
the scenery poor. I had seen the play a month before in London,
with the same beautiful artist in the chief part. Two years had
passed since, seeing her for the first time, I had hoped that she,
perhaps, might be the long-sought mystery. It had proved otherwise. On this night I looked at her and listened to her for the sake
of that bygone hope, and applauded her generously when the
curtain fell. But I went out lonely still. When I had supped at a
restaurant, I returned to my hotel, and tried to read. In vain. The
sound of feet in the corridors as the other occupants of the hotel
went to bed distracted my attention from my book. Suddenly it
occurred to me that I had never quite understood my uncle's
character. He, father to a great flock of poor and ignorant Irish;

an austere and saintly man, to whom livers of hopeless lives daily appealed for help heavenward; who was reputed never to have sent away a troubled peasant without relieving him of his burden by sharing it; whose knees were worn less by the altar steps than by the tears and embraces of the guilty and wretched: *he* had refused to humour my light extravagances, or to find time to talk with me of books, flowers, and music. Had I not been mad to expect it? Now that I needed sympathy myself, I did him justice. I desired to be with a true-hearted man, and to mingle my tears with his.

I looked at my watch. It was nearly an hour past midnight. In the corridor the lights were out, except one jet at the end. I threw a cloak upon my shoulders, put on a Spanish hat, and left my apartment, listening to the echoes of my measured steps retreating through the deserted passages. A strange sight arrested me on the landing of the grand staircase. Through an open door I saw the moonlight shining through the windows of a saloon in which some entertainment had recently taken place. I looked at my watch again: it was but one o'clock and yet the guests had departed. I entered the room, my boots ringing loudly on the waxed boards. On a chair lay a child's cloak and a broken toy. The entertainment had been a children's party. I stood for a time looking at the shadow of my cloaked figure upon the floor, and at the disordered decorations, ghostly in the white light. Then I saw that there was a grand piano, still open, in the middle of the room. My fingers throbbed as I sat down before it, and expressed all that I felt in a grand hymn which seemed to thrill the cold stillness of the shadows into a deep hum of approbation, and to people the radiance of the moon with angels. Soon there was a stir without too, as if the rapture were spreading abroad. I took up the chant triumphantly with my voice, and the empty saloon resounded as though to the thunder of an orchestra.

'Hallo, sir!' 'Confound you, sir—' 'Do you suppose that this—' 'What the deuce—?'

I turned; and silence followed. Six men, partially dressed, and with dishevelled hair, stood regarding me angrily. They all carried candles. One of them had a bootjack, which he held like a truncheon. Another, the foremost, had a pistol. The night porter was behind trembling.

'Sir,' said the man with the revolver, coarsely, 'may I ask

whether you are mad, that you disturb people at this hour with such an unearthly noise?'

'Is it possible that you dislike it?' I replied, courteously.

'Dislike it!' said he, stamping with rage. 'Why—damn everything—do you suppose we were enjoying it?'

'Take care: he's mad,' whispered the man with the bootjack.

I began to laugh. Evidently they did think me mad. Unaccustomed to my habits, and ignorant of music as they probably were, the mistake, however absurd, was not unnatural. I rose. They came closer to one another; and the night porter ran away.

'Gentlemen,' I said, 'I am sorry for you. Had you lain still and listened, we should all have been the better and happier. But what you have done, you cannot undo. Kindly inform the night porter that I am gone to visit my uncle, the Cardinal Archbishop. Adieu!'

I strode past them, and left them whispering among themselves. Some minutes later I knocked at the door of the Cardinal's house. Presently a window on the first floor was opened; and the moonbeams fell on a grey head, with a black cap that seemed ashy pale against the unfathomable gloom of the shadow beneath the stone sill.

'Who are you?'

'I am Zeno Legge.'

'What do you want at this hour?'

The question wounded me. 'My dear uncle,' I exclaimed, 'I know you do not intend it, but you make me feel unwelcome. Come down and let me in, I beg.'

'Go to your hotel,' he said sternly. 'I will see you in the morning. Goodnight.' He disappeared and closed the window.

I felt that if I let this rebuff pass, I should not feel kindly towards my uncle in the morning, nor, indeed, at any future time. I therefore plied the knocker with my right hand, and kept the bell ringing with my left until I heard the door-chain rattle within. The Cardinal's expression was grave nearly to moroseness as he confronted me on the threshold.

'Uncle,' I cried, grasping his hand, 'do not reproach me. Your door is never shut against the wretched. I am wretched. Let us sit up all night and talk.'

'You may thank my position and not my charity for your admission, Zeno,' he said. 'For the sake of the neighbours, I had rather you played the fool in my study than upon my doorstep at this hour. Walk upstairs quietly, if you please. My housekeeper is a hard-working woman: the little sleep she allows herself must not be disturbed.'

'You have a noble heart, uncle. I shall creep like a mouse.'

'This is my study,' he said, as we entered an ill-furnished den on the second floor. 'The only refreshment I can offer you, if you desire any, is a bunch of raisins. The doctors have forbidden you to touch stimulants, I believe.'

'By heaven—!' He raised his finger. 'Pardon me: I was wrong to swear. But I had totally forgotten the doctors. At dinner I had a bottle of *Graves*.'

'Humph! You have no business to be travelling alone. Your mother promised me that Bushy should come over here with you.'

'Pshaw! Bushy is not a man of feeling. Besides, he is a coward. He refused to come with me because I purchased a revolver.'

'He should have taken the revolver from you, and kept to his post.'

'Why will you persist in treating me like a child, uncle? I am very impressionable, I grant you; but I have gone round the world alone, and do not need to be dry-nursed through a tour in Ireland.'

'What do you intend to do during your stay here?'

I had no plans; and instead of answering I shrugged my shoulders and looked round the apartment. There was a statuette of the Virgin upon my uncle's desk. I looked at its face, as he was wont to look in the midst of his labours. I saw there eternal peace. The air became luminous with an infinite network of the jewelled rings of Paradise descending in roseate clouds upon us.

'Uncle,' I said, bursting into the sweetest tears I had ever shed, 'my wanderings are over. I will enter the Church, if you will help me. Let us read together the third part of *Faust*; for I understand it at last.'

'Hush, man,' he said, half rising with an expression of alarm. 'Control yourself.'

'Do not let my tears mislead you. I am calm and strong. Quick, let us have Goethe:

> Das Unbeschreibliche,
> Hier ist gethan;
> Das Ewig-Weibliche,
> Zieht uns hinan.'

'Come, come. Dry your eyes and be quiet. I have no library here.'

'But I have—in my portmanteau at the hotel,' I said, rising. 'Let me go for it, I will return in fifteen minutes.'

'The devil is in you, I believe. Cannot—'

I interrupted him with a shout of laughter. 'Cardinal,' I said noisily, 'you have become profane; and a profane priest is always the best of good fellows. Let us have some wine; and I will sing you a German beer song.'

'Heaven forgive me if I do you wrong,' he said; 'but I believe God has laid the expiation of some sin on your unhappy head. Will you favour me with your attention for a while? I have something to say to you, and I have also to get some sleep before my hour for rising, which is half-past five.'

'My usual hour for retiring—when I retire at all. But proceed. My fault is not inattention, but over-susceptibility.'

'Well, then, I want you to go to Wicklow. My reasons—'

'No matter what they may be,' said I, rising again. 'It is enough that you desire me to go. I shall start forthwith.'

'Zeno! will you sit down and listen to me?'

I sank upon my chair reluctantly. 'Ardour is a crime in your eyes, even when it is shown in your service,' I said. 'May I turn down the light?'

'Why?'

'To bring on my sombre mood, in which I am able to listen with tireless patience.'

'I will turn it down myself. Will that do?'

I thanked him, and composed myself to listen in the shadow. My eyes, I felt, glittered. I was like Poe's raven.

'Now for my reasons for sending you to Wicklow. First, for your own sake. If you stay in town, or in any place where excitement can be obtained by any means, you will be in Swift's Hospital in a week. You must live in the country, under the eye of one upon whom I can depend. And you must have something to do to keep you out of mischief, and away from your music and painting and poetry, which, Sir John Richards writes to me, are dangerous for you in your present morbid state. Second, because I can entrust you with a task which, in the hands of a sensible man, might bring discredit on the Church. In short, I want you to investigate a miracle.'

He looked attentively at me. I sat like a statue.

'You understand me?' he said.

'Nevermore,' I replied, hoarsely. 'Pardon me,' I added, amused at the trick my imagination had played me, 'I understand you perfectly. Proceed.'

'I hope you do. Well, four miles distant from the town of Wicklow is a village called Four Mile Water. The resident priest is Father Hickey. You have heard of the miracles at Knock?'

I winked.

'I did not ask you what you think of them, but whether you have heard of them. I see you have. I need not tell you that even a miracle may do more harm than good to the Church in this country, unless it can be proved so thoroughly that her powerful and jealous enemies are silenced by the testimony of followers of their heresy. Therefore, when I saw in a Wexford newspaper last week a description of a strange manifestation of the Divine Power which was said to have taken place at Four Mile Water, I was troubled in my mind about it. So I wrote to Father Hickey, bidding him give me an account of the matter if it were true, and, if not, to denounce from the altar the author of the report, and to contradict it in the paper at once. This is his reply. He says—well, the first part is about Church matters: I need not trouble you with it. He goes on to say—'

'One moment. Is that his own handwriting? It does not look like a man's.'

'He suffers from rheumatism in the fingers of his right hand; and his niece, who is an orphan, and lives with him, acts as his amanuensis. Well—'

'Stay. What is her name?'

'Her name? Kate Hickey.'

'How old is she?'

'Tush, man, she is only a little girl. If she were old enough to concern you, I should not send you into her way. Have you any more questions to ask about her?'

'None. I can fancy her in a white veil at the rite of confirmation, a type of faith and innocence. Enough of her. What says the Reverend Hickey of the apparitions?'

'They are not apparitions. I will read you what he says. Ahem! "In reply to your inquiries concerning the late miraculous event in this parish, I have to inform you that I can vouch for its truth, and that I can be confirmed not only by the inhabitants of the place, who are all Catholics, but by every person acquainted with the former situation of the graveyard referred to, including the Protestant Archdeacon of Baltinglas, who spends six weeks annually in the neighbourhood. The newspaper account is incomplete and inaccurate. The following are the facts: About four years ago, a man named Wolfe Tone Fitzgerald settled in this village as a farrier. His antecedents did not transpire; and he had no family. He lived by himself; was very careless of his person; and when in his cups, as he often was, regarded the honour neither of God nor man in his conversation. Indeed if it were not speaking ill of the dead, one might say that he was a dirty, drunken, blasphemous blackguard. Worse again, he was, I fear, an atheist; for he never attended Mass, and gave His Holiness worse language even than he gave the Queen. I should have mentioned that he was a bitter rebel, and boasted that his grandfather had been out in '98, and his father with Smith O'Brien. At last he went by the name of Brimstone Billy, and was held up in the village as the type of all wickedness.

'"You are aware that our graveyard, situate on the north side of the water, is famous throughout the country as the burial-place of the nuns of St Ursula, the hermit of Four Mile Water, and many other holy people. No Protestant has ever ventured to enforce his legal right of interment there, though two have died in the parish within my own recollection. Three weeks ago, this Fitzgerald died in a fit brought on by drink; and a great hullabaloo was raised in the village when it became known that he would be buried in the graveyard. The body had to be watched to prevent its being stolen and buried at the cross-roads. My people were greatly disappointed when they were told I could do nothing to stop the burial, particularly as I of course refused to read any service on the occasion. However, I bade them not interfere; and the interment was effected on the 14th of July, late in the evening, and long after the legal hour. There was no disturbance. Next morning, the graveyard was found moved to the south side of the water, with the one newly-filled grave left behind on the north side; and thus they both remain. The departed saints would not lie with the reprobate. I can testify to it on the oath of a Christian priest; and if this will not satisfy those outside the Church, everyone, as I said before, who remembers where the graveyard was two months ago, can confirm me.

'"I respectfully suggest that a thorough investigation into the truth of this miracle be proposed to a committee of Protestant gentlemen. They shall not be asked to accept a single fact on hearsay from my people. The ordnance maps show where the graveyard was; and anyone can see for himself where it is. I need not tell your Eminence what a rebuke this would be to those enemies of the holy Church that have sought to put a stain on her by discrediting the late wonderful manifestations at Knock Chapel. If they come to Four Mile Water, they need cross-examine no one. They will be asked to believe nothing but their own senses.

'"Awaiting your Eminence's counsel to guide me further in the matter,

'"I am, etc."'

'Well, Zeno,' said my uncle: 'what do you think of Father Hickey now?'

'Uncle: do not ask me. Beneath this roof I desire to believe everything. The Reverend Hickey has appealed strongly to my love of legend. Let us admire the poetry of his narrative, and ignore the balance of probability between a Christian priest telling a lie on his oath and a graveyard swimming across a river in the middle of the night and forgetting to return.'

'Tom Hickey is not telling a lie, sir. You may take my word for that. But he may be mistaken.'

'Such a mistake amounts to insanity. It is true that I myself, awaking suddenly in the depth of night, have found myself convinced that the position of my bed had been reversed. But on opening my eyes the illusion ceased. I fear Mr Hickey is mad. Your best course is this. Send down to Four Mile Water a perfectly sane investigator; an acute observer; one whose perceptive faculties, at once healthy and subtle, are absolutely unclouded by religious prejudice. In a word, send me. I will report to you the true state of affairs in a few days; and you can then make arrangements for transferring Hickey from the altar to the asylum.'

'Yes, I had intended to send you. You are wonderfully sharp; and you would make a capital detective if you could only keep your mind to one point. But your chief qualification for this business is that you are too crazy to excite the suspicion of those whom you may have to watch. For the affair may be a trick. If so, I hope and believe that Hickey has no hand in it. Still, it is my duty to take every precaution.'

'Cardinal: may I ask whether traces of insanity have ever appeared in our family?'

'Except in you and in my grandmother, no. She was a Pole; and you resemble her personally. Why do you ask?'

'Because it has often occurred to me that you are, perhaps, a little cracked. Excuse my candour; but a man who has devoted his life to the pursuit of a red hat; who accuses everyone else beside himself of being mad; and who is disposed to listen seriously to a tale of a peripatetic graveyard, can hardly be quite sane. Depend upon it, uncle, you want rest and change. The blood of your Polish grandmother is in your veins.'

'I hope I may not be committing a sin in sending a ribald on the Church's affairs,' he replied, fervently. 'However, we must use the instruments put into our hands. Is it agreed that you go?'

'Had you not delayed me with this story, which I might as well have learned on the spot, I should have been there already.'

'There is no occasion for impatience, Zeno. I must first send to Hickey to find a place for you. I shall tell him that you are going to recover your health, as, in fact, you are. And, Zeno, in Heaven's name be discreet. Try to act like a man of sense. Do not dispute with Hickey on matters of religion. Since you are my nephew, you had better not disgrace me.'

'I shall become an ardent Catholic, and do you infinite credit, uncle.'

'I wish you would, although you would hardly be an acquisition to the Church. And now I must turn you out. It is nearly three o'clock; and I need some sleep. Do you know your way back to your hotel!'

'I need not stir. I can sleep in this chair. Go to bed, and never mind me.'

'I shall not close my eyes until you are safely out of the house. Come, rouse yourself, and say goodnight.'

*　　*　　*

The following is a copy of my first report to the Cardinal:

Four Mile Water, County Wicklow,
10th August.

My Dear Uncle,

The miracle is genuine. I have affected perfect credulity in order to throw the Hickeys and the countryfolk off their guard with me. I have listened to their method of convincing sceptical strangers. I have examined the ordnance maps, and cross-examined the neighbouring Protestant gentlefolk. I have spent a day upon the ground on each side of the water, and have visited it at midnight. I have considered the upheaval theories, subsidence theories, volcanic theories and tidal wave theories which the provincial *savants* have suggested. They are all untenable. There is only one scoffer in the district, an Orangeman; and he admits the removal of the cemetery, but says it was dug up and transplanted in the night by a body of men under the command of Father Tom. This also is out of the question. The interment of Brimstone Billy was the first which had taken place for four years; and his is the only grave which bears a trace of recent digging. It is alone on the north bank; and the inhabitants shun it after nightfall. As each passer-by during the day throws a stone upon it, it will soon be marked by a large cairn. The graveyard, with a ruined stone chapel still standing in its midst, is on the south side. You may send down a committee to investigate the matter as soon as you please. There can be no doubt as to the miracle having actually taken place, as recorded by Hickey. As for me, I have grown so accustomed to it that if the county Wicklow were to waltz off with me to Middlesex, I should be quite impatient of any expressions of surprise from my friends in London.

Is not the above a businesslike statement? Away, then, with this stale miracle. If you would see for yourself a miracle which can never pall, a vision of youth and health to be crowned with garlands for ever, come down and see Kate Hickey, whom you suppose to be a little girl. Illusion, my lord cardinal, illusion! She is seventeen, with a bloom and a brogue that would lay your asceticism in ashes at a flash. To her I am an object of wonder, a strange man bred in wicked cities. She is courted by six feet of farming material, chopped off a spare length of coarse humanity by the Almighty, and flung into Wicklow to plough the fields. His name is Phil Langan; and he hates me. I have to consort with him for the sake of Father Tom, whom I entertain vastly by stories of your wild oats sown at Salamanca. I exhausted all my authentic anecdotes the first day; and now I invent gallant escapades with Spanish donnas, in which you figure as a youth of unstable morals. This delights Father Tom infinitely. I feel that I have done you a service by thus casting on the cold sacerdotal abstraction which formerly represented you in Kate's imagination a ray of vivifying passion.

What a country this is! A Hesperidean garden: such skies! Adieu, uncle.

Zeno Legge.

Behold me, then, at Four Mile Water, in love. I had been in love frequently; but not oftener than once a year had I encountered a woman who affected me as seriously as Kate Hickey. She was so shrewd, and yet so flippant! When I spoke of art she yawned. When I deplored the sordidness of the world she laughed, and called me 'poor fellow'! When I told her what a treasure of beauty and freshness she had she ridiculed me. When I reproached her with her brutality she became angry, and sneered at me for being what she called a fine gentleman. One sunny afternoon we were standing at the gate of her uncle's house, she looking down the dusty road for the detestable Langan, I watching the spotless azure sky, when she said:

'How soon are you going back to London?'

'I am not going back to London, Miss Hickey. I am not yet tired of Four Mile Water.'

'I'm sure Four Mile Water ought to be proud of your approbation.'

'You disapprove of my liking it, then? Or is it that you grudge me the happiness I have found there? I think Irish ladies grudge a man a moment's peace.'

'I wonder you have ever prevailed on yourself to associate with Irish ladies, since they are so far beneath you.'

'Did I say they were beneath me, Miss Hickey? I feel that I have made a deep impression on you.'

'Indeed! Yes, you're quite right. I assure you I can't sleep at night for thinking of you, Mr Legge. It's the best a Christian can do, seeing you think so mighty little of yourself.'

'You are triply wrong, Miss Hickey: wrong to be sarcastic with me, wrong to pretend that there is anything unreasonable in my belief that you think of me sometimes, and wrong to discourage the candour with which I always avow that I think constantly of myself.'

'Then you had better not speak to me, since I have no manners.'

'Again! Did I say you had no manners? The warmest expressions of regard from my mouth seem to reach your ears transformed into insults. Were I to repeat the Litany of the Blessed Virgin, you would retort as though I had been reproaching you. This is because you hate me. You never misunderstand Langan, whom you love.'

'I don't know what London manners are, Mr Legge; but in Ireland gentlemen are expected to mind their own business. How dare you say I love Mr Langan?'

'Then you do not love him?'

'It is nothing to you whether I love him or not.'

'Nothing to me that you hate me and love another?'

'I didn't say I hated you. You're not so very clever yourself at understanding what people say, though you make such a fuss because they don't understand you.' Here, as she glanced down the road again, she suddenly looked glad.

'Aha!' I said.

'What do you mean by "Aha!"'

'No matter. I will now show you what a man's sympathy is. As you perceived just then, Langan—who is too tall for his age, by the bye—is coming to pay you a visit. Well, instead of staying with you, as a jealous woman would, I will withdraw.'

'I don't care whether you go or stay, I'm sure. I wonder what you would give to be as fine a man as Mr Langan.'

'All I possess: I swear it! But solely because you admire tall men more than broad views. Mr Langan may be defined geometrically as length without breadth; altitude without position; a line on the landscape, not a point in it.'

'How very clever you are!'

'You do not understand me, I see. Here comes your lover, stepping over the wall like a camel. And here go I, out through the gate like a Christian. Good afternoon, Mr Langan. I am going because Miss Hickey has something to say to you about me which she would rather not say in my presence. You will excuse me?'

'Oh, I'll excuse you,' said he boorishly. I smiled, and went out. Before I was quite out of hearing, Kate whispered vehemently to him, 'I *hate* that fellow.'

I smiled again; but I had scarcely done so when my spirits fell. I walked hastily away with a coarse threatening sound in my ears like that of the clarionets whose sustained low notes darken the woodland in 'Der Freischütz'. I found myself presently at the graveyard. It was a barren place, enclosed by a mud wall with a gate to admit funerals, and numerous gaps to admit the peasantry, who made short cuts across it as they went to and fro between Four Mile Water and the market town. The graves were mounds overgrown with grass: there was no keeper; nor were there flowers, railings or any of the conventionalities that make an English grave-yard repulsive. A great thorn bush, near what was called the grave of the holy sisters, was covered with scraps of cloth and flannel, attached by peasant women who had prayed before it. There were three kneeling there as I entered; for the reputation of the place had been revived of late by the miracle; and a ferry had been established close by, to conduct visitors over the route taken by the graveyard. From where I stood I could see on the opposite bank the heap of stones, perceptibly increased since my last visit, marking the deserted grave of Brimstone Billy. I strained my eyes broodingly at it for some minutes, and then descended the river bank and entered the boat.

'Good evenin t'your honour,' said the ferryman, and set to work to draw the boat hand over hand by a rope stretched across the water.

'Good evening. Is your business beginning to fall off yet?'

'Faith, it never was as good as it mightabeen. The people that comes from the south side can see Billy's grave—Lord have mercy on him!—across the wather; and they think bad of payin' a penny to put a stone over him. It's them that lives towrst Dublin that makes the journey. Your honour is the third I've brought from south to north this blessed day.'

'When do most people come? In the afternoon, I suppose?'

'All hours, sur, except afther dusk. There isnt a sowl in the counthry ud come within sight of that grave wanst the sun goes down.'

'And you! do you stay here all night by yourself?'

'The holy heavens forbid! Is it me stay here all night? No, your honour: I tether the boat at siven o'hlyock, and lave Brimstone Billy—God forgimme!—to take care of it t'll mornin'.'

'It will be stolen some night, I'm afraid.'

'Arra, who'd dar come next or near it, let alone stale it? Faith, I'd think twice before lookin' at it meself in the dark. God bless your honour, and gran'che long life.'

I had given him sixpence. I went to the reprobate's grave and stood at the foot of it, looking at the sky, gorgeous with the descent of the sun. To my English eyes, accustomed to giant trees, broad lawns, and stately mansions, the landscape was wild and inhospitable. The ferryman was already tugging at the rope on his way back (I had told him I did not intend to return that way), and presently I saw him make the painter fast to the south bank; put on his coat; and trudge homeward. I turned towards the grave at my feet. Those who had interred Brimstone Billy, working hastily at an unlawful hour, and in fear of molestation by the people, had hardly dug a grave. They had scooped out earth enough to hide their burden, and no more. A stray goat had kicked away a corner of the mound and exposed the coffin. It occurred to me, as I took some of the stones from the cairn, and heaped them so as to repair the breach, that had the miracle been the work of a body of men, they would have moved the one grave instead of the many. Even from a supernatural point of view, it seemed strange that the sinner should have banished the elect, when, by their superior numbers, they might so much more easily have banished him.

It was almost dark when I left the spot. After a walk of half a mile, I recrossed the water by a bridge, and returned to the farmhouse in which I lodged. Here, finding that I had had enough of solitude, I only stayed to take a cup of tea. Then I went to Father Hickey's cottage.

Kate was alone when I entered. She looked up quickly as I opened the door, and turned away disappointed when she recognised me.

'Be generous for once,' I said. 'I have walked about aimlessly for hours in order to avoid spoiling the beautiful afternoon for you by my presence. When the sun was up I withdrew my shadow from your path. Now that darkness has fallen, shed some light on mine. May I stay half an hour?'

'You may stay as long as you like, of course. My uncle will soon be home. He is clever enough to talk to you.'

'What! More sarcasms! Come, Miss Hickey, help me to spend a pleasant evening. It will only cost you a smile. I am somewhat cast down. Four Mile Water is a paradise; but without you, it would be a little lonely.'

'It must be very lonely for you. I wonder why you came here.'

'Because I heard that the women here were all Zerlinas, like you, and the men Masettos, like Mr Phil—where are you going to?'

'Let me pass, Mr Legge. I had intended never speaking to you again after the way you went on about Mr Langan today; and I wouldn't either, only my uncle made me promise not to take any notice of you, because you were—no matter; but I won't listen to you any more on the subject.'

'Do not go. I swear never to mention his name again. I beg your pardon for what I said: You shall have no further cause for complaint. Will you forgive me?'

She sat down, evidently disappointed by my submission. I took a chair, and placed myself near her. She tapped the floor impatiently with her foot. I saw that there was not a movement I could make, not a look, not a tone of my voice, which did not irritate her.

'You were remarking,' I said, 'that your uncle desired you to take no notice of me because—'

She closed her lips, and did not answer.

'I fear I have offended you again by my curiosity. But indeed, I had no idea that he had forbidden you to tell me the reason.'

'He did not forbid me. Since you are so determined to find out—'

'No: excuse me. I do not wish to know, I am sorry I asked.'

'Indeed! Perhaps you would be sorrier still to be told. I only made a secret of it out of consideration for you.'

'Then your uncle has spoken ill of me behind my back. If that be so, there is no such thing as a true man in Ireland. I would not have believed it on the word of any woman alive save yourself.'

'I never said my uncle was a backbiter. Just to show you what he thinks of you, I will tell you, whether you want to know it or

not, that he bid me not mind you because you were only a poor
mad creature, sent down here by your family to be out of harm's
way.'

'Oh, Miss Hickey!'

'There now! you have got it out of me; and I wish I had bit my
tongue out first. I sometimes think—that I maytr't sin!—that you
have a bad angel in you.'

'I am glad you told me this,' I said gently. 'Do not reproach
yourself for having done so, I beg. Your uncle has been misled by
what he has heard of my family, who are all more or less insane.
Far from being mad, I am actually the only rational man named
Legge in the three kingdoms. I will prove this to you, and at the
same time keep your indiscretion in countenance, by telling you
something I ought not to tell you. It is this. I am not here as an
invalid or a chance tourist. I am here to investigate the miracle.
The Cardinal, a shrewd if somewhat erratic man, selected mine
from all the long heads at his disposal to come down here, and
find out the truth of Father Hickey's story. Would he have
entrusted such a task to a madman, think you?'

'The truth of—who dared to doubt my uncle's word? And so
you are a spy, a dirty informer.'

I started. The adjective she had used, though probably the com-
monest expression of contempt in Ireland, is revolting to an Eng-
lishman.

'Miss Hickey,' I said: 'there is in me, as you have said, a bad
angel. Do not shock my good angel—who is a person of taste—
quite away from my heart, lest the other be left undisputed monarch of it. Hark! The chapel bell is ringing the angelus. Can you,
with that sound softening the darkness of the village night, cherish
a feeling of spite against one who admires you?'

'You come between me and my prayers,' she said hysterically,
and began to sob. She had scarcely done so, when I heard voices
without. Then Langan and the priest entered.

'Oh, Phil,' she cried, running to him, 'take me away from him:
I can't bear—' I turned towards him, and showed him my dog-
tooth in a false smile. He felled me at one stroke, as he might
have felled a poplar-tree.

'Murdher!' exclaimed the priest. 'What are you doin', Phil?'

'He's an informer,' sobbed Kate. 'He came down here to spy
on you, uncle, and to try and show that the blessed miracle was

a make-up. I knew it long before he told me, by his insulting ways. He wanted to make love to me.'

I rose with difficulty from beneath the table, where I had lain motionless for a moment.

'Sir,' I said, 'I am somewhat dazed by the recent action of Mr Langan, whom I beg, the next time he converts himself into a fulling-mill, to do so at the expense of a man more nearly his equal in strength than I. What your niece has told you is partly true. I am indeed the Cardinal's spy; and I have already reported to him that the miracle is a genuine one. A committee of gentlemen will wait on you tomorrow to verify it, at my suggestion. I have thought that the proof might be regarded by them as more complete if you were taken by surprise. Miss Hickey: that I admire all that is admirable in you is but to say that I have a sense of the beautiful. To say that I love you would be mere profanity. Mr Langan: I have in my pocket a loaded pistol, which I carry from a silly English prejudice against your countrymen. Had I been the Hercules of the ploughtail, and you in my place, I should have been a dead man now. Do not redden: you are safe as far as I am concerned.'

'Let me tell you before you leave my house for good,' said Father Hickey, who seemed to have become unreasonably angry, 'that you should never have crossed my threshold if I had known you were a spy: no, not if your uncle were his Holiness the Pope himself.'

Here a frightful thing happened to me. I felt giddy, and put my hand to my head. Three warm drops trickled over it. Instantly I became murderous. My mouth filled with blood, my eyes were blinded with it; I seemed to drown in it. My hand went involuntarily to the pistol. It is my habit to obey my impulses instantaneously. Fortunately the impulse to kill vanished before a sudden perception of how I might miraculously humble the mad vanity in which these foolish people had turned upon me. The blood receded from my ears; and I again heard and saw distinctly.

'And let *me* tell you,' Langan was saying, 'that if you think yourself handier with cold lead than you are with your fists, I'll exchange shots with you, and welcome, whenever you please. Father Tom's credit is the same to me as my own; and if you say a word against it, you lie.'

'His credit is in my hands,' I said. 'I am the Cardinal's witness. Do you defy me?'

'There is the door,' said the priest, holding it open before me. 'Until you can undo the visible work of God's hand your testimony can do no harm to me.'

'Father Hickey,' I replied, 'before the sun rises again upon Four Mile Water, I will undo the visible work of God's hand, and bring the pointing finger of the scoffer upon your altar.'

I bowed to Kate, and walked out. It was so dark that I could not at first see the garden-gate. Before I found it, I heard through the window Father Hickey's voice, saying, 'I wouldn't for ten pound that this had happened, Phil. He's as mad as a march hare. The Cardinal told me so.'

I returned to my lodging, and took a cold bath to cleanse the blood from my neck and shoulder. The effect of the blow I had received was so severe, that even after the bath and a light meal I felt giddy and languid. There was an alarm-clock on the mantel-piece: I wound it; set the alarm for half-past twelve; muffled it so that it should not disturb the people in the adjoining room; and went to bed, where I slept soundly for an hour and a quarter. Then the alarm roused me, and I sprang up before I was thoroughly awake. Had I hesitated, the desire to relapse into per-fect sleep would have overpowered me. Although the muscles of my neck were painfully stiff, and my hands unsteady from my nervous disturbance, produced by the interruption of my first slum-ber, I dressed myself resolutely, and, after taking a draught of cold water, stole out of the house. It was exceedingly dark; and I had some difficulty in finding the cow-house, whence I borrowed a spade, and a truck with wheels, ordinarily used for moving sacks of potatoes. These I carried in my hands until I was beyond earshot of the house, when I put the spade on the truck, and wheeled it along the road to the cemetery. When I approached the water, knowing that no one would dare to come thereabout at such an hour, I made greater haste, no longer concerning myself about the rattling of the wheels. Looking across to the opposite bank, I could see a phosphorescent glow, marking the lonely grave of Brimstone Billy. This helped me to find the ferry station, where, after wandering a little and stumbling often, I found the boat, and embarked with my implements. Guided by the rope, I crossed the water without difficulty; landed; made fast the boat; dragged the truck up the bank; and sat down to rest on the cairn at the grave. For nearly a quarter of an hour I sat watching the patches of jack-o'-lantern fire, and collecting my strength for the work before me. Then the distant bell of the chapel clock tolled one. I rose; took the spade; and in about ten minutes uncovered the coffin, which smelt horribly. Keeping to windward of it, and using the spade as a lever, I contrived with great labour to place it on the truck. I wheeled it without accident to the landing-place, where, by placing the shafts of the truck upon the stern of the boat and lifting the foot by main strength, I succeeded in embarking my load after twenty minutes' toil, during which I got covered with clay and perspiration, and several times all but upset the boat. At the southern bank I had less difficulty in getting truck and coffin ashore, and dragging them up to the graveyard.

It was now past two o'clock, and the dawn had begun; so that I had no further trouble from want of light. I wheeled the coffin to a patch of loamy soil which I had noticed in the afternoon near the grave of the holy sisters. I had warmed to my work; my neck no longer pained me; and I began to dig vigorously, soon making a shallow trench, deep enough to hide the coffin with the addition of a mound. The chill pearl-coloured morning had by this time quite dissipated the darkness. I could see, and was myself visible, for miles around. This alarmed me, and made me impatient to finish my task. Nevertheless, I was forced to rest for a moment before placing the coffin in the trench. I wiped my brow and wrists, and again looked about me. The tomb of the holy women, a massive slab supported on four stone spheres, was grey and wet with dew. Near it was the thornbush covered with rags, the newest of which were growing gaudy in the radiance which was stretching up from the coast on the east. It was time to finish my work. I seized the truck; laid it alongside the grave; and gradually prised the coffin off with the spade until it rolled over into the trench with a hollow sound like a drunken remonstrance from the sleeper within. I shovelled the earth round and over it, working as fast as possible. In less than a quarter of an hour it was buried. Ten minutes more sufficed to make the mound symmetrical, and to clear the traces of my work from the adjacent sward. Then I flung down the spade; threw up my arms; and vented a sigh of relief and triumph. But I recoiled as I saw that I was standing on a barren common, covered with furze. No product of man's handiwork was near me except my truck and spade and the grave of Brimstone Billy, now as lonely as before. I turned towards the water. On the opposite bank was the cemetery, with the tomb of the holy women, the thornbush with its rags stirring in the morning breeze, and the broken mud wall. The ruined chapel was there too, not a stone shaken from its crumbling walls, not a sign to show that it and its precinct were less rooted in their place than the eternal hills around.

I looked down at the grave with a pang of compassion for the unfortunate Wolfe Tone Fitzgerald, with whom the blessed would not rest. I was even astonished, though I had worked expressly to this end. But the birds were astir, and the cocks crowing. My landlord was an early riser. I put the spade on the truck again, and hastened back to the farm, where I replaced them in the cow-house. Then I stole into the house, and took a clean pair of boots, an overcoat, and a silk hat. These, with a change of linen, were sufficient to make my appearance respectable. I went out again, bathed in the Four Mile Water, took a last look at the cemetery, and walked to Wicklow, whence I travelled by the first train to Dublin.

*   *   *

Some months later, at Cairo, I received a packet of Irish newspapers and a leading article, cut from *The Times*, on the subject of the miracle. Father Hickey had suffered the meed of his inhospitable conduct. The committee, arriving at Four Mile Water the day after I left, had found the graveyard exactly where it had formerly stood. Father Hickey, taken by surprise, had attempted to defend himself by a confused statement, which led the committee to declare finally that the miracle was a gross imposture. *The Times*, commenting on this after adducing a number of examples of priestly craft, remarked, 'We are glad to learn that the Rev. Mr Hickey has been permanently relieved of his duties as the parish priest of Four Mile Water by his ecclesiastical superior. It is less gratifying to have to record that it has been found possible to obtain two hundred signatures to a memorial embodying the absurd defence offered to the committee, and expressing unabated confidence in the integrity of Mr Hickey.'

FIVE POUNDS OF FLESH

J. M. Synge

*   *   *

When I was going out this morning to walk round the island with Michael, the boy who is teaching me Irish, I met an old man making his way down to the cottage. He was dressed in miserable black clothes which seemed to have come from the mainland, and was so bent with rheumatism that, at a little distance, he looked more like a spider than a human being.

Michael told me it was Pat Dirane, the storyteller old Mourteen had spoken of on the other island. I wished to turn back, as he appeared to be on his way to visit me, but Michael would not hear of it.

'He will be sitting by the fire when we come in,' he said: 'let you not be afraid, there will be time enough to be talking to him by and by.'

He was right. As I came down into the kitchen some hours later old Pat was still in the chimney-corner, blinking with the turf-smoke.

He spoke English with remarkable aptness and fluency, due, I believe, to the months he spent in the English provinces working at the harvest when he was a young man.

After a few formal compliments he told me how he had been crippled by an attack of the 'old hin' (i.e., the influenza), and had been complaining ever since in addition to his rheumatism.

While the old woman was cooking my dinner he asked me if I liked stories, and offered to tell one in English, though, he added, it would be much better if I could follow the Gaelic. Then he began:

There were two farmers in County Clare. One had a son, and the other, a fine rich man, had a daughter.

The young man was wishing to marry the girl, and his father told him to try and get her if he thought well, though a power of gold would be wanting to get the like of her.

'I will try,' said the young man.

He put all his gold into a bag. Then he went over to the other farm, and threw in the gold in front of him.

'Is that all gold?' said the father of the girl.

'All gold,' said O'Conor (the young man's name was O'Conor).

'It will not weigh down my daughter,' said the father.

'We'll see that,' said O'Conor.

Then they put them in a scales, the daughter in one side and the gold in the other. The girl went down against the ground, so O'Conor took his bag and went out on the road.

As he was going along he came to where there was a little man, and he standing with his back against the wall.

'Where are you going with the bag?' said the little man.

'Going home,' said O'Conor.

'Is it gold you might be wanting?' said the man.

'It is, surely,' said O'Conor.

'I'll give you what you are wanting,' said the man, 'and we can bargain in this way—you'll pay me back in a year the gold I give you, or you'll pay me with five pounds cut off your own flesh.'

That bargain was made between them. The man gave a bag of gold to O'Conor, and he went back with it, and was married to the young woman.

They were rich people, and he built her a grand castle on the cliffs of Clare, with a window that looked out straightly over the wild ocean.

One day when he went up with his wife to look out over the wild ocean, he saw a ship coming in on the rocks, and no sails on her at all. She was wrecked on the rocks, and it was tea that was in her, and fine silk.

O'Conor and his wife went down to look at the wreck, and when the lady O'Conor saw the silk she said she wished a dress of it.

They got the silk from the sailors, and when the Captain came up to get the money for it, O'Conor asked him to come again and take his dinner with them. They had a grand dinner, and they drank after it, and the Captain was tipsy. While they were still drinking, a letter came to O'Conor, and it was in the letter than a friend of his was dead, and that he would have to go away on a long journey. As he was getting ready the Captain came to him.

'Are you fond of your wife?' said the Captain.

'I am fond of her,' said O'Conor.

'Will you make me a bet of twenty guineas no man comes near her while you'll be away on the journey?' said the Captain.

'I will bet it,' said O'Conor, and he went away.

There was an old hag who sold small things on the road near the castle, and the lady O'Conor allowed her to sleep up in her room in a big box. The Captain went down on the road to the old hag.

'For how much will you let me sleep one night in your box?' said the Captain.

'For no money at all would I do such a thing,' said the hag.

'For ten guineas?' said the Captain.

'Not for ten guineas,' said the hag.

'For twelve guineas?' said the Captain.

'Not for twelve guineas,' said the hag.

'For fifteen guineas?' said the Captain.

'For fifteen I will do it,' said the hag.

Then she took him up and hid him in the box. When night came the lady O'Conor walked up into her room, and the Captain watched her through a hole that was in the box. He saw her take off her two rings and put them on a kind of board that was over her head like a chimney-piece, and take off her clothes, except her shift, and go up into her bed.

As soon as she was asleep the Captain came out of his box, and he had some means of making a light, for he lit the candle. He went over to the bed where she was sleeping without disturbing her at all, or doing any bad thing, and he took the two rings off the board, and blew out the light, and went down again into the box.

He paused for a moment, and a deep sigh of relief rose from the men and women who had crowded in while the story was going on, till the kitchen was filled with people.

As the Captain was coming out of his box the girls, who had appeared to know no English, stopped their spinning and held their breath with expectation.

The old man went on—

When O'Conor came back the Captain met him, and told him that he had been a night in his wife's room, and gave him the two rings.

O'Conor gave him the twenty guineas of the bet. Then he went up into the castle, and he took his wife up to look out of the window over the wild ocean. While she was looking he pushed her from behind, and she fell down over the cliff into the sea.

An old woman was on the shore, and she saw her falling. She went down then to the surf and pulled her out all wet and in great disorder, and she took the wet clothes off of her, and put on some old rags belonging to herself.

When O'Conor had pushed his wife from the window he went away into the land.

After a while the lady O'Conor went out searching for him, and when she had gone here and there a long time in the country, she heard that he was reaping in a field with sixty men.

She came to the field and she wanted to go in, but the gate-man would not open the gate for her. Then the owner came by, and she told him her story. He brought her in, and her husband was there, reaping, but he never gave any sign of knowing her. She showed him to the owner, and he made the man come out and go with his wife.

Then the lady O'Conor took him out on the road where there were horses, and they rode away.

When they came to the place where O'Conor had met the little man, he was there on the road before them.

'Have you my gold on you?' said the man.

'I have not,' said O'Conor.

'Then you'll pay me the flesh off your body,' said the man.

They went into a house, and a knife was brought, and a clean white cloth was put on the table, and O'Conor was put upon the cloth.

Then the little man was going to strike the lancet into him, when says lady O'Conor—

'Have you bargained for five pounds of flesh?'

'For five pounds of flesh,' said the man.

'Have you bargained for any drop of his blood?' said lady O'Conor.

'For no blood,' said the man.

'Cut out the flesh,' said lady O'Conor, 'but if you spill one drop of his blood I'll put that through you.' And she put a pistol to his head.

The little man went away, and they saw no more of him.

When they got home to their castle they made a great supper, and they invited the Captain and the old hag, and the old woman that had pulled the lady O'Conor out of the sea.

After they had eaten well the lady O'Conor began, and she said they would all tell their stories. Then she told how she had been saved from the sea, and how she had found her husband.

Then the old woman told her story, the way she had found the lady O'Conor wet, and in great disorder, and had brought her in and put on her some old rags of her own.

The lady O'Conor asked the Captain for his story, but he said they would get no story from him. Then she took her pistol out of her pocket, and she put it on the edge of the table, and she said that any one that would not tell his story would get a bullet into him.

Then the Captain told the way he had got into the box, and come over to her bed without touching her at all, and had taken away the rings.

Then the lady O'Conor took the pistol and shot the hag through the body, and they threw her over the cliff into the sea.

THE WATCHER O' THE DEAD

John Guinan

*   *   *

It is now the fall of the night. The last of the neighbours are hitting the road for home. The time they went out through that door together, for the sake of the company on the way, as they said, did they give e'er a thought at all to myself, left alone here in this desolate house? To be sure, they asked me more than once why I refuse to leave the place, and the day is in it, by the same token. But I have no call to answer them, though what I am about to set down here in black and white will settle the question, at least for myself.

A few hours ago, and the corpse of Tim McGowan was taken from under this roof and buried deep in the clay. They laid the spade and the shovel like a rude cross on the fresh sod of his grave, and they went down on their knees and said a few hasty prayers for the good of his soul. One or two, and their faces hidden in their hats, took good care not to rise from the wet ground till they got sight of others already on their two feet. Letting on that their thoughts were on higher things, they kept in mind the old belief that the first one to leave the churchyard warm in life would not be the last to come back cold in death.

The little groups moving out began to talk of the man who was gone. Their talk ran in whispers, for fear they might trouble his long sleep. They all knew, though none had the rights of it, that he was after earning his rest dearly. An old man, whose face was hard, even for his years, took a white clay pipe from the pocket of his body coat.

'God rest your soul, Tim McGowan,' he cried. It was the custom to pray for the dead before taking a 'draw' from a wake pipe. 'God rest you in the grave,' he added, 'for it's little peace or ease you had and you in the world that we know!'

The bulk of those who heard his words caught, a little gladly, a mocking undertone which stole through the kindly feeling that had at first shaken his voice. A young man, with eager eyes and a desire to know and talk of things that should be left hidden, took courage and spoke out bluntly:

'For him to be haunting the graveyard like a ghost, and he a living man! That was a strange vagary, for sure.'

'It was the death of the good woman a year ago,' the old man went on, speaking more openly, in his turn. 'It was her loss turned his poor head.'

'There's no denying there was a queer strain in him already,' the young man said to that. 'Sure they say all of that family were a bit touched!'

They did not scruple to speak like this before myself, and I of the one blood with the man who was dead, if any of them could know or suspect that. They were after doing their duty towards his mortal remains: if there was a kink in his nature or a mystery about his life why, they might fairly ask, should it not fill the gossip of the idle hour? But it was myself only, the stranger amongst them, who knew the true reason of Tim McGowan's nightly vigils in Gort na Marbh, why he, a living man, as was said, chose to become the Watcher o' the Dead in the lonesome graveyard. It was ere yesterday morning he told me his secret. Tim was lying there in the settle-bed from which his stark body was carried feet foremost this day. I was trying to get ready a little food by the fire on the hearth, for Tim had not been able to rise, let alone to do a hand's turn for himself. Our wants were simple, and it was not for the first time that I had turned my poor endeavours to homely use.

'There are times,' I made bold to remark, 'there are times I feel this house to be haunted': for every night during the short spell since I came to see my kinsman, I was sure I heard the fall of footsteps on the floor after the pair of us had gone to our beds. The rattling of the door, if it was not a troubled dream, had also startled me in my sleep. I had begun to ask myself was it one of these houses where the door must be left on the latch and the hearth swept clean for Those who come back. Always at a certain hour Tim was in a hurry to rake the fire and get shut of me out of the kitchen. A pang now shot through my breast. With the poor man hardly able to raise hand or foot, it was not kind to draw down such a thing. But he looked glad that I had given him the chance to speak out.

'As you make mention of it,' he said eagerly, 'I want to let you know the house is haunted, surely! But it is not by any spirit of good or evil from beyond the grave. That is a strange thing, you will be saying.'

'It is a strange thing,' I agreed. I had no doubt what he was going to disclose. He had already given me the story of a house built, and not without warning, on a 'fairy pass', through which the Sluagh Sidhe in their hosting and revels swept gaily every night. This was the house for sure: The Gentle Folk had never passed the gates of death and know nothing of the grave.

'But,' he went on, 'there is one other thing as strange again. It is that same you will now be hearing, if you pay heed to me.'

'You mean that this is the house'—I began, intending to say that it was the house of the story, but I checked myself—'that it is a case of a fallen angel, hanging between heaven and hell, who never had to pay the penalty of death?'

'If you let me,' he made answer, 'I will tell you the truth. The place is haunted by a mortal man!'

'One still in the world, one who goes about in his clothes, one to be seen by daylight?' I asked, without drawing breath.

'In troth,' he declared, 'it is haunted by the man who tells it, and no other, if I am still in the flesh itself!'

I lifted him slightly in the bed, not knowing what to say or think. Was this his way of speaking about some common habit, or was his reason leaving him?

'Whisper!' he said, and his face was flushed. 'You came here to gather old stories out of the past, over and above seeing your last living relative in the world, leaving our Michael, my son, who should be here by this. I might do worse than give you the true version of my own trouble.'

This made a double reason why I should hear him out. There is no man but carries in his breast the makings of a story, which, though never told, comes more home to him than any the mind of another man can find and fashion in words.

'What harm if my story should turn out a poor thing in the telling?' he sighed. 'It will ease my mind, if it does only that. And who knows: but we will talk of that when the time comes.'

He turned aside from the food I was coaxing him to take, and started:

'It is now a year since herself was laid to rest. Laid to rest!' He laughed, a little bitterly. 'That is what they call it. A week after that again, call it what you like, the graveyard was closed by orders. There are people still to the fore who have their rights under the law; but it is hardly likely that many, if any of them, will try to make good their claim to be buried in Gort na Marbh.'

Gurthnamorrav, the Field of the Dead, that is what those around about call the lonely patch to this day. Though this generation of them are 'dull of' the ancient tongue, such names, of native savour, help to keep them one in soul with the proud children of Banbha who are in eternity. Vivid imagery, symbols drawn, in a manner of speaking, from the brown earth, words of strength and beauty that stud like gems of light and grace the common speech hold not merely an abiding charm in themselves. Such heritages of the mind of the Gael evoke through active fancy the fuller life of the race of kings no less surely than those relics of skill and handcraft found by chance in tilth or red bog, the shrine of bell or battle book, the bronze spear head, the torque of gold.

'But, surely,' I objected, 'those who are able would like to have their bones laid beside their own when their day of nature is past! Surely they would choose such a ground as the place of their resurrection, as the holy men of old used to say!'

'Time and time again,' he made answer, 'people have left it to their deaths not to be buried in Gort na Marbh. Man and wife have been parted, mother and child. What call have I to tell you the reason? You know it rightly. You know it is the lot of the last body brought to its long home to be from that time forth the Watcher o' the Dead?'

'I have heard tell of that queer—of that belief,' I replied. 'That the poor soul cannot go to its rest, if it took years itself, till another comes to fill its place; that it must wander about in the dead of the night amongst the graves where the mortal body is crumbling to dust; and, as one might say in a plain way, keep an eye over the place!'

'And who would care to be buried in ground that was shut up for ever?' he asked. 'Even at the best of times people try their best endeavours to be first through the gate with the corpse of their own friend and when two funerals happen to fall on the one day.'

And then he went on to tell me, and his voice failing at that, of all he was after going through thinking of his woman, his share of the world, making the weary, dreary, rounds of the graveyard during the best part of the changing year. And, bitter agony! he felt that she could not share in the Communion of Saints, that all his good works for her sake would not hasten her release. But the thing that made it the hardest for him to bear was this: It was through his veneration for the old customs, through his great respect even for the dead, that this awful tribulation had come to the pair of them.

'Let you not be laughing at what I'm going to tell you now,' he warned me: 'for I won't deny there have been times when I made merry over the like myself. It was a seldom thing two funerals to be the one day; nor would it have come to happen at the time it did if the other people had the proper spirit, like myself, or the right regard for the things good Christians hold highly. Listen! They knew the order to close the graveyard, the other people knew it was on the road, for the man who was dead and going to be buried on the same day as herself was himself on the Board of Guardians. That was why they waked him for one night only, and they people of means, and rushed with him in unseemly haste to Gort na Marbh. But we got wind of it, and would have been the first, for all that, only we followed the old road, the long road, and in a decent and becoming way walked in through the open gate while they took a short cut and got in over the stile. We did more than that, and so did they. While the savages, for they were little less, while they were trampling above the relics of the dead, we went round about the ground in the track of the sun till we came in the proper course to the side of the open grave.'

This set me thinking of the ancient ritual by which the corpse is brought round to pay its respects, as a body might say, to those who have gone before. I began to ask myself was it a fragment of Druid worship that had come down even to our own day. But this is what I said to my kinsman:

'You did what was right, and no one would be better pleased than the woman who was gone!'

'That is the way I felt myself at the first going off,' he agreed: 'but soon I began to question myself: When I did the right thing, that the neighbours gave me full credit for, was I thinking more of what was expected from the living or what was due to the dead? Was I thinking of myself, and the great name I'd be getting from the self-same neighbours, or of the woman going into the clay, who only wanted their prayers? Many's the long night this thought kept me on the rack till I was nigh gone astray in the head. In my mind I saw her, and her brown habit down to her feet, and she looking to me for help, and it my sin of human respect, as I felt, that kept her so long from walking on the sunny hills of Glory! Funeral after funeral went the way, for people have to die; but not a one but passed the rusty gate of Gort na Marbh as a poor woman of the road might give the go-by to a stricken house.

'At length and at last, I could stand it no longer, and one night I got up from my bed and made my way to the graveyard. 'Twas in the dark hour before the crowing of the cocks, when wandering spirits are warned home to their house of clay.'

'And did you half expect to see the Watcher o' the Dead?' I asked.

'Did I? And why not?' he asked in turn, by way of reply.

'With your mind disturbed that way,' I went on, 'the wonder is you didn't see her, if only in fancy.'

I meant to be kind. He faced me testily.

'I did see her, as sure as I'm a living man!' he declared.

I had not the heart to urge my view that it was only a brain-born figure.

'I no sooner crossed the stile,' he said softly, 'than I got clear sight of herself. She was moving through the graves she guarded, and a kindly look in her two eyes. The dead image I thought her of the Nuns you see in the sick ward of the poorhouse in Ballybrosna, and she taking a look at the beds in their little rows, and fearing to waken the tired sleepers in her charge. There she was, in truth, as I had seen her a thousand times in my own mind.'

'In your own mind!' I said after him. 'It was on your eyes, so to speak, and you merely saw what was in your mind already. Was it not more natural to see the figment that never left your sight than not to see it at all?'

It was all very clear to me, and I felt this was sound talk; and isn't it a caution the way the rage of battle will rise in a body and set the tongue loose! But Tim's reply put a stop to any dispute or war of words.

'It was in my mind, for sure,' he said. 'But tell me, you who have the book learning, why was it in my mind? When a man's brain begins to work, what gives it the start, or sets it going—or does it start to go of itself?'

I had to give in that I always left such vexed questions to wiser heads, adding, whimsically enough as it seems to me now, that I was not such a great fool as to attempt an answer where they failed. In a way I was put out by the reflection that this old man, who 'didn't know his letters', was making a mockery of me on the head of my few books and my small store of book learning.

'There is nothing hard about the case I am after putting before you,' he said. 'It was on my mind because the thing was taking place in Gort an Marbh night after night, was taking place in the Field of the Dead, though there was no living eye to see it!'

I had no reply to that, whether it was a head-made ghost or not. Where was the use of starting to argue that nothing really takes place if not within the knowledge of man? I told myself weakly that such visions were due to the queer strain in the old man the neighbours spoke about this day. It might be that, in his present state, all this had only come into his head as the two of us talked together. It did not occur to me then, and I have too much respect for the dead to credit it now, that he was 'taking a rise' out of me, as the plain saying is.

Tim became a little rambling in his speech and asked me to let him lie flat in the bed. I gathered from the words he mumbled and jumbled that he made a promise to the departed spirit to take her place till his own time came in real earnest: that he had bid her go to her rest, in the Name of God, much, I could not help but think, as one might banish an evil spirit to the 'red sea' to make ropes of the sand; that he had kept his word, which brought great peace to his breast: and that he never set eyes on her again from that hour, there or there else.

I had no doubt he had but laid the ghost of his own troubled thoughts. It is not every poor mortal can do that same, even by dint of hard sacrifice. Tim was growing worse. I tried hard to cheer him. It was all to no use. I talked of his son, Michael, who was far away on the fishing grounds. We had already sent word for him to come home, and he might be here any stroke, if it was a long ways off, itself.

'Michael will never be here in time!' the father groaned. 'That is my great trouble. I never could ask another to do it. It would be again' reason.'

'There is nothing you could name I would not gladly do!' I declared; and, in all fair speaking, I meant it.

'There are things no man should ask of his friend,' he said to that, with a slight shake of the head.

'And who else should he ask but his friend?' I laughed, trying to rouse him. 'But, first, I'll send for the Doctor—'

'The Doctor, how are ye!' he broke in on me. 'That is not what I want. What can the like of himself do for a body who has seen the Watcher o' the Dead?'

'What hark if you did itself?' I asked. 'The sign of a long life it is, as likely as not. It would be another story, entirely, one's "fetch" to be seen in the late hours of the day. An early death that would signify.'

'The man,' he made answer, 'the man who lays eyes on the Watcher o' the Dead, late or early, if the like could come to pass at all before dark, that man will soon be only a shadow himself. I am saying, he will soon be among the silent company. The time

I took the woman's place, the woman who held my heart for years, I knew rightly, it would not be for long. It is for that reason and no other I am after telling you my secret sorrow. I will never be able to put out this night, if I live through this night of the nights, or any night for the future; and if it was a thing I failed her, sure herself would be disturbed in her rest.'

I took a grip of his hand and looked down steadily into his eyes.

'Put your trust in me!' I said. 'I'll take your place till such time as you are laid in the clay!'

Who is it, though he might throw doubt on the very stars above his head, would not try to humour an old man or a little child?

'God sent you for a friend,' he said, 'praised be His holy Name! For all I know, I may not want you to do so much: I may want you to do a little more, but in another way. I want you to take my place till Michael comes, and not an hour more; I want you, as well as that, to tell him all I have told you and to give him my dying wish, if it is a thing he does not come before I go for ever. Whisper! You'll tell Michael, in case I'm too far through myself, that I am dying happy knowing he will not refuse a last favour to the father who reared him. It is this: That he will become the Watcher o' the Dead, though a living man, like myself, and let me, after so much fret and torment, go straight to herself, to his mother, in Heaven. Tell him I know he will do this, for the rest of his mortal days, if it comes to that. Tell him I know that, after that again, if he gets no release he will have his bones laid in Gort na Marbh and wait his own turn. I have done my share of watching, God knows!'

Some kind neighbours gathered during the course of the day, and the priest of the parish was sent for. Father Malachy was a man of the world, without being worldly. It is not for the knowing, and never will be in this world, whether Tim told him about the Watcher o' the Dead. As a man, his reverence knew all the customs and beliefs of the people, for he was one of them himself. Deep in his nature a body might expect to find a kindly toleration for the harmless 'superstitions', as some would call them, lingering from the pagan days of Firbolg or Tuatha de Danaan. As a priest, he had, no doubt, full knowledge of the rites of the Church for dealing with 'appearances' from the other world, which shows it to be no harm to give heed to such things.

Tim kept quiet till the night wore on. Then he got restless and began to mutter to himself. The use of his speech was wellnigh gone. I caught such words as 'Gort na Marbh', and 'Herself', and 'the Watcher o' the Dead'. His grip was tight on my fist when I said in his ear that I would not fail him, dead or alive, till Michael came. The kind neighbours did not let on to hear the pair of us, and I left him in their charge while I set out for the strange duty I had taken on myself so lightly, taken on, indeed, with a certain zest, in the vague hope of enlarging my experience. It was clear from Tim's behaviour that the hour of the night had come when he felt the 'call' to the graveyard, and still there was no sign of Michael. The moon was in the sky. The night was cold. There was no stir. The place held no terrors for me. I set little store by Tim's story, except as a 'study' in delusion. The old man was much in my thoughts, for he was passing rapidly away. I saw him in my mind, as he used to say, and he walking here and there through the graves that now held nothing but cold clay, passing by fallen stones, broken and moss-grown. I tried hard to banish such airy pictures, for I did not want to begin seeing sights.

What was that story Tim told me a few days ago as we stood before a headstone in Gort na Marbh? It was a true tale of revenge, revenge both on the living and the dead, and it was a poor sort of revenge at that. Before long I would be seeing again the spot where the dead man he spoke about was laid in the clay. His relations, in blood and law, hoped to benefit largely by his death. But he left all to his son. The boy was an only child whose mother died the hour he came into the world. He came home, a likely youth, to be at the father's funeral. For the first time in his young life he saw the place that was now to be his own. It was natural for him to ask why the usual black plumes did not wave above the hearse instead of white. The errors of the past, if any, should have been covered by charity. Feuds are forgiven, if not forgotten, in the hour of death. It is what they told him, with wild malice, that black plumes were only for people who were lawfully joined in wedlock.

Here I found the elements of tragedy, but the story only helped to keep the figure of Tim before me. I was stepping over the stile and thinking of the nights he spent walking about in the dreary waste, for, after so much neglect, that is what it had by now sunk to. I felt the nettles rank and dank as I set foot on the ground; and then—if it was not wild phantasy!—I got sight of Tim moving in the moonlight among the shadows of the headstones and the trees.

'In the Name of God!' I cried, profanely, I am half afraid, 'leave the place at once, and let me keep my promise in peace.'

I was furious with the neighbours for letting him rise and he in a fever. But were they to be blamed? I crossed hastily and found myself alone! This gave me a start, and I began to wonder whether in that strange ground—for, surely, the place was not 'right'!—I, in my turn, saw what was on my eyes only? Had Tim been there in the flesh or was it that I, in my turn, had laid but the ghost of a deranged imagination? Could it be that the queer strain of the family, if there is such a thing, runs in my own blood? Or does a sane man put such a question to himself? Without waiting for the crowing of the cocks, I made haste back to the house. My heart was beating loudly.

'We were going to call after you,' the neighbours said to me. 'Hardly was your back turned when the end came!'

Tim was stretched there in his long sleep, his features set free by the kindly touch of death!

Last night at the same hour we dug his grave. I was heartened by the presence of the neighbours and lingered over the work till the dawn broke, walking about from time to time, 'by way of no harm', trying to keep my promise to the dead man. More than once the shadows, moving with the shifting lanthorn, took a start out of me. There were a few of the neighbours would not put out with us. One was the strong young man who was so free of the tongue this day.

'Why do you want to choose such an unreasonable hour?' they grumbled. 'It is not lucky to turn up the sod in the dead of the night.'

'As likely as not,' I heard another make answer, 'he was waiting to see would Michael come on the long car.'

I did not put him right. If we were waiting for Michael only the work could have been left over till morning. It is the long wait we would have, for the same Michael, God rest the poor boy! God rest him! I say, for before Tim was taken out this day word came that the hardy young fisherman had been lost a week ago in the depths of the salt water. The hungry, angry sea did not give up its dead. And now his death comes home to me! Michael's bones will never be laid in Gort na Marbh. Michael will never, never, either in life or death, become the Watcher o' the Dead! And I have pledged my word to the man who is gone, the father, to take his place till such time as Michael should come home! That will be never, never!

What way can I break my word to the dead, whether I credit his story or doubt it? It was part of his own belief, part of himself. What odds does it make even if he was out of his mind, or if I am a madman myself? A promise, a promise to one passed away, is sacred.

Where is the good of talking of common sense! Half the world is stupid with common sense, if there is any such quality. But I see a dismal prospect before me, till the end of my days, as likely as not, let alone, for all I know, till the Day of Judgement itself! Already I feel there is a stir in my blood, the time has come for me to get up and make my lonely vigil: for I have been putting this down in black and white for many hours. It is a true word for Tim; every man has his own story, his own agony. But I set out to tell of his troubles, which, for sure, are at an end, and not of my own, which, for all a body can see, are only in their birth throes.

FOOTSTEPS IN THE LOBBY

Joseph Sheridan Le Fanu

*   *   *

I went to my room early that night, but I was too miserable to sleep. At about twelve o'clock, feeling very nervous, I determined to call my cousin Emily, who slept in the next room, which communicated with mine by a second door. By this private entrance I found my way into her chamber, and without difficulty persuaded her to return to my room and sleep with me. We accordingly lay down together—she undressed, and I with my clothes on—for I was every moment walking up and down the room, and felt too nervous and miserable to think of rest or comfort. Emily was soon fast asleep, and I lay awake, fervently longing for the first pale gleam of morning, reckoning every stroke of the old clock with an impatience which made every hour appear like six.

It must have been about one o'clock when I thought I heard a slight noise at the partition door between Emily's room and mine, as if caused by somebody's turning the key in the lock. I held my breath, and the same sound was repeated at the second door of my room—that which opened upon the lobby—the sound was here distinctly caused by the revolution of the bolt in the lock, and it was followed by a slight pressure upon the door itself, as if to ascertain the security of the lock. The person, whoever it might be, was probably satisfied, for I heard the old boards of the lobby creak and strain, as if under the weight of somebody moving cautiously over them.

My sense of hearing became unnaturally, almost painfully acute. I suppose the imagination added distinctness to sounds vague in themselves. I thought that I could actually hear the breathing of the person who was slowly returning down the lobby; at the head of the staircase there appeared to occur a pause; and I could distinctly hear two or three sentences hastily whispered; the steps then descended the stairs with apparently less caution. I now ventured to walk quickly and lightly to the lobby door, and attempted to open it; but it was indeed fast locked upon the outside, as was also the other. I now felt that the dreadful hour was come; but one desperate expedient remained—it was to awaken Emily, and by our united strength, to attempt to force the partition door, which was slighter than the other, and through this to pass to the lower part of the house, whence it might be possible to escape to the grounds, and forth to the village.

I returned to the bedside, and shook Emily, but in vain; nothing that I could do availed to produce from her more than a few incoherent words—it was a death-like sleep. She had certainly drunk of some narcotic, as had I probably also, in spite of all the caution with which I had examined everything presented to us to eat or drink. I now attempted, with as little noise as possible, to force first one door, then the other—but all in vain. I believe no strength could have effected my object, for both doors opened inwards. I therefore collected whatever movables I could carry thither, and piled them against the doors, so as to assist me in whatever attempts I should make to resist the entrance of those without. I then returned to the bed and endeavoured again, but fruitlessly, to awaken my cousin. It was not sleep, it was torpor, lethargy, death. I knelt down and prayed with an agony of earnestness; and then seating myself upon the bed, I awaited my fate with a kind of terrible tranquillity.

I heard a faint clanking sound from the narrow court below, as if caused by the scraping of some iron instrument against stones or rubbish. I at first determined not to disturb the calmness which

I now felt, by uselessly watching the proceedings of those who sought my life; but as the sounds continued, the horrible curiosity which I felt overcame every other emotion, and I determined, at all hazards, to gratify it. I therefore crawled upon my knees to the window, so as to let the smallest portion of my head appear above the sill.

The moon was shining with an uncertain radiance upon the antique grey buildings, and obliquely upon the narrow court beneath, one side of which was therefore clearly illuminated, while the other was lost in obscurity, the sharp outlines of the old gables, with their nodding clusters of ivy, being at first alone visible. Whoever or whatever occasioned the noise which had excited my curiosity, was concealed under the shadow of the dark side of the quadrangle. I placed my hand over my eyes to shade them from the moonlight, which was so bright as to be almost dazzling, and, peering into the darkness, I first dimly, but afterwards gradually, almost with full distinctness, beheld the form of a man engaged in digging what appeared to be a rude hole close under the wall. Some implements, probably a shovel and pickaxe, lay beside him, and to these he every now and then applied himself as the nature of the ground required. He pursued his task rapidly, and with as little noise as possible.

'So,' thought I, as shovelful after shovelful the dislodged rubbish mounted into a heap, 'they are digging the grave in which, before two hours pass, I must lie, a cold, mangled corpse. I am *theirs*— I cannot escape.' I felt as if my reason was leaving me. I started to my feet, and in mere despair I applied myself again to each of the two doors alternately. I strained every nerve and sinew, but I might as well have attempted, with my single strength, to force the building itself from its foundation. I threw myself madly upon the ground, and clasped my hands over my eyes as if to shut out the horrible images which crowded upon me.

The paroxysm passed away. I prayed once more with the bitter, agonised fervour of one who feels that the hour of death is present and inevitable. When I arose I went once more to the window and looked out, just in time to see a shadowy figure glide stealthily along the wall. The task was finished. The catastrophe of the tragedy must soon be accomplished. I determined now to defend my life to the last; and that I might be able to do so with some effect, I searched the room for something which might serve as a weapon;

but either through accident, or from an anticipation of such a possibility, everything which might have been made available for such a purpose had been carefully removed. I must thus die tamely and without an effort to defend myself.

A thought suddenly struck me—might it not be possible to escape through the door, which the assassin must open in order to enter the room? I resolved to make the attempt. I felt assured that the door through which ingress to the room would be effected was that which opened upon the lobby. It was the more direct way, besides being, for obvious reasons, less liable to interruption than the other. I resolved then to place myself behind a projection of the wall, whose shadow would serve fully to conceal me, and when the door should be opened, and before they should have discovered the identity of the occupant of the bed, to creep noise-lessly from the room, and then to trust to Providence for escape. In order to facilitate this scene, I removed all the lumber which I had heaped against the door; and I had nearly completed my arrangements, when I perceived the room suddenly darkened by the close approach of some shadowy object to the window. On turning my eyes in that direction, I observed at the top of the casement, as if suspended from above, first the feet, then the legs, then the body, and at length the whole figure of a man present itself.

It was Edward T——n. He appeared to be guiding his descent so as to bring his feet upon the centre of the stone block which occupied the lower part of the window; and having secured his footing upon this, he kneeled down and began to gaze into the room. As the moon was gleaming into the chamber, and the bed curtains were drawn, he was able to distinguish the bed itself and its contents. He appeared satisfied with his scrutiny, for he looked up and made a sign with his hand, upon which the rope by which his descent had been effected was slackened from above, and he proceeded to disengage it from his waist: this accomplished, he applied his hands to the window-frame, which must have been ingeniously contrived for the purpose, for with apparently no resistance the whole frame, containing casement and all, slipped from its position in the wall, and was by him lowered into the room. The cold night waved the bed-curtains, and he paused for a moment—all was still again—and he stepped in upon the floor of the room. He held in his hand what appeared to be a steel instrument, shaped something like a hammer, but larger and sharper at the extremities. This he held rather behind him, while, with three long *tip-toe* strides, he brought himself to the bedside.

I felt that the discovery must now be made, and held my breath in momentary expectation of the execration in which he would vent his surprise and disappointment. I closed my eyes—there was a pause—but it was a short one. I heard two dull blows, given in rapid succession: a quivering sigh, and the long-drawn, heavy breathing of the sleeper was for ever suspended. I unclosed my eyes, and saw the murderer fling the quilt across the head of his victim: he then, with the instrument of death still in his hand, proceeded to the lobby door, upon which he tapped sharply twice or thrice—a quick step was then heard approaching, and a voice whispered something from without—Edward answered, with a kind of chuckle, 'Her ladyship is past complaining; unlock the door, in the devil's name, unless you're afraid to come in, and help me to lift the body out of the window.' The key was turned in the lock—the door opened—and my uncle entered the room.

I have told you already that I had placed myself under the shade of a projection of the wall, close to the door. I had instinctively shrunk down cowering towards the ground on the entrance of Edward through the window. When my uncle entered the room, he and his son both stood so very close to me that his hand was every moment upon the point of touching my face. I held my breath, and remained motionless as death.

'You had no interruption from the next room?' said my uncle.

'No,' was the brief reply.

'Secure the jewels, Ned; the French harpy must not lay her claws upon them. You've a steady hand, by G—; not much blood—eh?'

'Not twenty drops,' replied his son, 'and those on the quilt.'

'I'm glad it's over,' whispered my uncle again; 'we must lift the—the *thing* through the window, and lay the rubbish over it.'

They then turned to the bedside, and, winding the bed-clothes round the body, carried it between them slowly to the window, and, exchanging a few brief words with someone below, they shoved it over the window sill, and I heard it fall heavily on the ground underneath.

'I'll take the jewels,' said my uncle; 'there are two caskets in the lower drawer.'

He proceeded, with an accuracy which, had I been more at ease, would have furnished me with matter of astonishment, to lay his hand upon the very spot where my jewels lay; and having possessed himself of them, he called to his son—

'Is the rope made fast above?'

'I'm not a fool—to be sure it is,' replied he.

They then lowered themselves from the window. I now rose lightly and cautiously, scarcely daring to breathe, from my place of concealment, and was creeping towards the door, when I heard my cousin's voice, in a sharp whisper, exclaim, 'Scramble up again; G—d d—n you, you've forgot to lock the door;' and I perceived, by the straining of the rope which hung from above, that the mandate was instantly obeyed.

Not a second was to be lost. I passed through the door, which was only closed, and moved as rapidly as I could, consistently with stillness, along the lobby. Before I had gone many yards I heard the door through which I had just passed double locked on the inside. I glided down the stairs in terror, lest, at every corner, I should meet the murderer or one of his accomplices. I reached the hall, and listened for a moment to ascertain whether all was silent around; no sound was audible; the parlour windows opened on the park, and through one of them I might, I thought, easily effect my escape. Accordingly, I hastily entered; but, to my consternation, a candle was burning in the room, and by its light I saw a figure seated at the dinner-table, upon which lay glasses, bottles, and the other accompaniments of a drinking party.

There was no other means of escape, so I advanced with a firm step and collected mind to the window. I noiselessly withdrew the bars and unclosed the shutters—I pushed open the casement, and, without waiting to look behind me, I ran with my utmost speed, scarcely feeling the ground under me, down the avenue, taking care to keep upon the grass which bordered it. I did not for a moment slack my speed, and I had now gained the centre point between the park gate and the mansion-house—here the avenue made a wider circuit, and in order to avoid delay, I directed my way across the smooth sward round which the pathway wound, intending, at the opposite side of the flat, at a point which I distinguished by a group of old birch trees, to enter again upon the beaten track, which was from thence tolerably direct to the gate.

I had, with my utmost speed, got about halfway across this broad flat when the rapid treading of a horse's hoofs struck upon my ear. My heart swelled in my bosom, as though I would smother. The clattering of galloping hoofs approached—I was pursued— they were now upon the sward on which I was running—there was not a bush or a bramble to shelter me—and, as if to render escape altogether desperate, the moon, which had hitherto been obscured, at this moment shone forth with a broad clear light, which made every object distinctly visible. The sounds were now close behind me. I felt my knees bending under me, with the sensation which torments one in dreams. I reeled—I stumbled— I fell—and at the same instant the cause of my alarm wheeled past me at full gallop. It was one of the young fillies which pastured loose about the park, whose frolics had thus all but maddened me with terror.

I scrambled to my feet, and rushed on with weak but rapid steps, my sportive companion still galloping round and round me with many a frisk and fling, until, at length, more dead than alive, I reached the avenue gate and crossed the stile, I scarce knew how. I ran through the village, in which all was silent as the grave, until my progress was arrested by the hoarse voice of a sentinel, who cried, 'Who goes there?' I felt that I was now safe. I turned in the direction of the voice, and fell fainting at the soldier's feet.

When I came to myself I was sitting in a miserable hovel, sur- rounded by strange faces, all bespeaking curiosity and compassion. Many soldiers were in it also; indeed, as I afterwards found, it was employed as a guard-room by a detachment of troops quartered for that night in the town. In a few words I informed their officer of the circumstances which had occurred, describing also the appear- ance of the persons engaged in the murder; and he, without loss of time, proceeded to the mansion-house of Carrickleigh, taking with him a number of his men. But the villains had discovered their mistake, and had effected their escape, before the arrival of the military.

Deep and fervent as must always be my gratitude to Heaven for my deliverance, effected by a chain of providential occur- rences, the failing of a single link of which must have insured my destruction, I was long before I could look back upon it with other feelings than those of bitterness, almost of agony. My cousin, the only being that had ever really loved me, my nearest dearest friend, ever ready to sympathise, to counsel, and to assist—the gayest, the gentlest, the warmest heart—the only creature on earth that cared for me—*her* life had been the price of my deliverance; and I then uttered the wish—which no event of my long and sorrowful life has taught me to recall—that she had been spared, and that in her stead *I* were mouldering in the grave forgotten and at rest.

THE CEDAR CLOSET

Patrick Lafcadio Hearn

*   *   *

It happened ten years ago, and it stands out, and ever will stand out, in my memory like some dark, awful barrier dividing the happy, gleeful years of girlhood, with their foolish, petulant sorrows and eager, innocent joys, and the bright, lovely life which has been mine since. In looking back, that time seems to me shadowed by a dark and terrible brooding cloud, bearing in its lurid gloom what, but for love and patience the tenderest and most untiring, might have been the bolt of death, or, worse a thousand times, of madness. As it was, for months after 'life crept on a broken wing', if not 'through cells of madness', yet verily 'through haunts of horror and fear'. O, the weary, weary days and months when I longed piteously for rest! when sunshine was torture, and every shadow filled with horror unspeakable; when my soul's craving was for death; to be allowed to creep away from the terror which lurked in the softest murmur of the summer breeze, the flicker of the shadow of the tiniest leaf on the sunny grass, in every corner and curtain-fold in my dear old home. But love conquered all, and I can tell my story now, with awe and wonder, it is true, but quietly and calmly.

Ten years ago I was living with my only brother in one of the

126

quaint, ivy-grown, red-gabled rectories which are so picturesquely scattered over the fair breadth of England. We were orphans, Archibald and I; and I had been the busy, happy mistress of his pretty home for only one year after leaving school, when Robert Draye asked me to be his wife. Robert and Archie were old friends, and my new home, Draye's Court, was only separated from the parsonage by an old grey wall, a low iron-studded door in which admitted us from the sunny parsonage dawn to the old, old park which had belonged to the Drayes for centuries. Robert was lord of the manor; and it was he who had given Archie the living of Draye in the Wold.

It was the night before my wedding day, and our pretty home was crowded with the wedding guests. We were all gathered in the large old-fashioned drawing-room after dinner. When Robert left us late in the evening, I walked with him, as usual, to the little gate for what he called our last parting; we lingered awhile under the great walnut-tree, through the heavy, sombre branches of which the September moon poured its soft pure light. With his last goodnight kiss on my lips and my heart full of him and the love which warmed and glorified the whole world for me, I did not care to go back to share in the fun and frolic in the drawing-room, but went softly upstairs to my own room. I say 'my own room', but I was to occupy it as a bedroom tonight for the first time. It was a pleasant south room, wainscoted in richly-carved cedar, which gave the atmosphere a spicy fragrance. I had chosen it as my morning room on my arrival in our home; here I had read and sung and painted, and spent long, sunny hours while Archibald was busy in his study after breakfast. I had had a bed arranged there as I preferred being alone to sharing my own larger bedroom with two of my bridesmaids. It looked bright and cosy as I came in; my favourite low chair was drawn before the fire, whose rosy light glanced and flickered on the glossy dark walls, which gave the room its name, 'The Cedar Closet'. My maid was busy preparing my toilet table, I sent her away, and sat down to wait for my brother, who I knew would come to bid me goodnight. He came; we had our last fireside talk in my girlhood's home; and when he left me there was an incursion of all my bridesmaids for a 'dressing-gown reception.'

When at last I was alone I drew back the curtain and curled myself up on the low wide window-seat. The moon was at its brightest; the little church and quiet churchyard beyond the lawn looked fair and calm beneath its rays; the gleam of the white headstones here and there between the trees might have reminded me that life is not all peace and joy—that tears and pain, fear and parting, have their share in its story—but it did not. The tranquil happiness with which my heart was full overflowed in some soft tears which had no tinge of bitterness, and when at last I did lie down, peace, deep and perfect, still seemed to flow in on me with the moonbeams which filled the room, shimmering on the folds of my bridal dress, which was laid ready for the morning. I am thus minute in describing my last waking moments, that it may be understood that what followed was not creation of a morbid fancy.

I do not know how long I had been asleep, when I was suddenly, as it were, wrenched back to consciousness. The moon had set, the room was quite dark; I could just distinguish the glimmer of a clouded, starless sky through the open window. I could not see or hear anything unusual, but not the less was I conscious of an unwonted, a baleful presence near; an indescribable horror cramped the very beatings of my heart; with every instant the certainty grew that my room was shared by some evil being. I could not cry for help, though Archie's room was so close, and I knew that one call through the death-like stillness would bring him to me; all I could do was gaze, gaze, gaze into the darkness. Suddenly—and a throb stung through every nerve—I heard distinctly from behind the wainscot against which the head of my bed was placed a low, hollow moan, followed on the instant by a cackling, malignant laugh from the other side of the room. If I had been one of the monumental figures in the little churchyard on which I had seen the quiet moonbeams shine a few hours before I could not have been more utterly unable to move or speak; every other faculty seemed to be lost in the one intent strain of eye and ear. There came at last the sound of a halting step, the tapping of a crutch upon the floor, then stillness, and slowly, gradually the room filled with light—a pale, cold, steady light. Everything around was exactly as I had last seen it in the mingled shine of the moon and fire, and though I heard at intervals the harsh laugh, the curtain at the foot of the bed hid from me whatever uttered it. Again, low but distinct, the piteous moan broke forth, followed by some words in a foreign tongue, and with the sound a figure started from behind the curtain—a dwarfed, deformed woman, dressed in a loose robe of black, sprinkled with golden stars, which gave forth a dull, fiery gleam, in the mysterious light; one lean, yellow hand clutched the curtain of my bed; it glittered with jewelled rings;—long black hair fell in heavy masses from a golden circlet over the stunted form. I saw it all clearly as I now see the pen which writes these words and the hand which guides it. The face was turned from me, bent aside, as if greedily drinking in those astonished moans; I noted even the streaks of grey in the long tresses, as I lay helpless in dumb, bewildered horror.

'Again!' she said hoarsely, as the sounds died away into indistinct murmurs, and advancing a step she tapped sharply with a crutch on the cedar wainscot; then again louder and more purposeful rose the wild beseeching voice; this time the words were English.

'Mercy, have mercy! not on me, but on my child, my little one; she never harmed you. She is dying—she is dying here in darkness; let me but see her face once more. Death is very near, nothing can save her now; but grant one ray of light, and I will pray that you may be forgiven, if forgiveness there be for such as you.'

'What, you kneel at last! Kneel to Gerda, and kneel in vain. A ray of light! Not if you could pay for it in diamonds. You are mine! Shriek and call as you will, no other ears can hear. Die together. You are mine to torture as I will; mine, mine, mine!' and again an awful laugh rang through the room. At the instant she turned. O the face of malign horror that met my gaze! The green eyes flamed, and with something like the snarl of a savage beast she sprang towards me; that hideous face almost touched mine; the grasp of the skinny jewelled hand was all but on me; then—I suppose I fainted.

For weeks I lay in brain fever, in mental horror and weariness so intent, that even now I do not like to let my mind dwell on it. Even when the crisis was safely past I was slow to rally; my mind was utterly unstrung. I lived in a world of shadows. And so winter wore by, and brought us to the fair spring morning when at last I stood by Robert's side in the old church, a cold, passive, almost unwilling bride. I cared neither to refuse nor consent to anything that was suggested; so Robert and Archie decided for me, and I allowed them to do with me as they would, while I brooded silently and ceaselessly on the memory of that terrible night. To my husband I told all one morning in a sunny Bavarian valley, and my weak, frightened mind drew strength and peace from his; by degrees the haunting horror wore away, and when we came home for a happy reason nearly two years afterwards, I was as strong and blithe as in my girlhood. I had learned to believe that it had all been, not the cause, but the commencement of my fever. I was to be undeceived.

Our little daughter had come to us in the time of roses; and now Christmas was with us, our first Christmas at home, and the house was full of guests. It was a delicious old-fashioned Yule; plenty of skating and outdoor fun, and no lack of brightness indoors. Towards New Year a heavy fall of snow set in which kept us all prisoners; but even then the days flew merrily, and somebody suggested tableaux for the evenings. Robert was elected manager; there was a debate and selection of subjects, and then came the puzzle of where, at such short notice, we could procure the dresses required. My husband advised a raid on some mysterious oaken chests which we knew had been for years stowed away in a turret-room. He remembered having, when a boy, seen the housekeeper inspecting them, and their contents had left a hazy impression of old stand-alone brocades, gold tissues, sacques, hoops and hoods, the very mention of which put us in a state of wild excitement. Mrs Moultrie was summoned, looked duly horrified at the desecration of what to her were relics most sacred; but seeing it was inevitable, she marshalled the way, a protest in every rustle and fold of her stiff silk dress.

'What a charming old place,' was the exclamation with variations as we entered the long oak-joisted room, at the further end of which stood in goodly array the chests whose contents we coveted. Bristling with unspoken disapproval, poor Mrs Moultrie unlocked one after another, and then asked permission to retire, leaving us unchecked to 'cry havoc'. In a moment the floor was covered with piles of silks and velvets.

'Meg,' cried little Janet Crawford, dancing up to me, 'isn't it a good thing to live in the age of tulle and summer silks? Fancy being imprisoned for life in a fortress like this!' holding up a thick crimson and gold brocade, whaleboned and buckramed at all points. It was thrown aside, and she half lost herself in another chest and was silent. Then—'Look, Major Fraude! This is the very thing for you—a true astrologer's robe, all black velvet and golden stars. If it were but long enough; it just fits me.'

I turned and saw—the pretty slight figure, the innocent girlish face dressed in the robe of black and gold, identical in shape, pattern and material with what I too well remembered. With a wild cry I hid my face and cowered away.

'Take it off! O, Janet—Robert—take it from her!'

Every one turned wondering. In an instant my husband saw, and catching up the cause of my terror, flung it hastily into the chest again, and lowered the lid. Janet looked half offended, but the cloud passed in an instant when I kissed her, apologising as well as I could. Rob laughed at us both, and voted an adjournment to a warmer room, where we could have the chests brought to us to ransack at leisure. Before going down, Janet and I went into a small anteroom to examine some old pictures which leaned against the wall.

'This is just the thing, Jennie, to frame the tableaux,' I said, pointing to an immense frame, at least twelve feet square. 'There is a picture in it,' I added, pulling back the dusty folds of a heavy curtain which fell before it.

'That can be easily removed,' said my husband, who had followed us.

With his assistance we drew the curtain quite away, and in the now fast waning light could just discern the figure of a girl in white against a dark background. Robert rang for a lamp, and when it came we turned with much curiosity to examine the painting, as to the subject of which we had been making odd merry guesses while we waited. The girl was young, almost childish—very lovely, but, oh, how sad! Great tears stood in the innocent eyes and on the round young cheeks, and her hands were clasped tenderly around the arms of a man who was bending towards her, and, did I dream?—no, there in hateful distinctness was the hideous woman of the Cedar Closet—the same in every distorted line, even to the starred dress and golden circlet. The swarthy hues of the dress and the face had at first caused us to overlook her. The same wicked eyes seemed to glare into mine. After one wild bound my heart seemed to stop its beating, and I knew no more. When I recovered from a long, deep swoon, great lassitude and intense nervous excitement followed; my illness broke up the party, and for months I was an invalid. When again Robert's love and patience had won me back to my old health and happiness, he told me all the truth, so far as it had been preserved in old records of the family.

It was in the sixteenth century that the reigning lady of Draye

Court was a weird, deformed woman, whose stunted body, hideous face, and a temper which taught her to hate and vilify everything good and beautiful for the contrast offered to herself, made her universally feared and disliked. One talent only she possessed; it was for music; but so wild and strange were the strains she drew from the many instruments of which she was mistress, that the gift only intensified the dread with which she was regarded. Her father had died before her birth; her mother did not survive it; near relatives she had none; she had lived her lonely, loveless life from youth to middle age. When a young girl came to the Court, no one knew more than that she was a poor relation. The dark woman seemed to look more kindly on this young cousin than on anyone that had hitherto crossed her sombre path, and indeed so great was the charm which Marian's goodness, beauty and innocent gaiety exercised on everyone that the servants ceased to marvel at her having gained the favour of their gloomy mistress. The girl seemed to feel a kind of wondering, pitying affection for the unhappy woman; she looked on her through an atmosphere created by her own sunny nature, and for a time all went well. When Marian had been at the Court for a year, a foreign musician appeared on the scene. He was a Spaniard, and had been engaged by Lady Draye to build for her an organ said to be of fabulous power and sweetness. Through long bright summer days he and his employer were shut up together in the music-room—he busy in the construction of the wonderful instrument, she aiding and watching his work. These days were spent by Marian in various ways—pleasant idleness and pleasant work, long canters on her chestnut pony, dreamy mornings by the brook with rod and line, or in the village near, where she found a welcome everywhere. She played with the children, nursed the babies, helped the mothers in a thousand pretty ways, gossiped with old people, brightening the day for everybody with whom she came in contact. Then in the evening she sat with Lady Draye and the Spaniard in the saloon, talking in that soft foreign tongue which they generally used. But this was but the music between the acts; the terrible drama was coming. The motive was of course the same as that of every life drama which has been played out from the old, old days when the curtain rose upon the garden scene of Paradise. Philip and Marian loved each other, and having told their happy secret to each other, they, as in duty bound, took it to their patroness. They found her in the music room. Whether the glimpses she caught of a beautiful world from which she was shut out maddened her, or whether she, too, loved the foreigner, was never certainly known; but through the closed door passionate words were heard, and very soon Philip came out alone, and left the house without a farewell to any in it. When the servants did at last venture to enter, they found Marian lifeless on the floor, Lady Draye standing over her with crutch uplifted, and blood flowing from a wound in the girl's forehead. They carried her away and nursed her tenderly; their mistress locked the door as they left, and all night long remained alone in darkness. The music which came out without pause on the still night air was weird and wicked beyond any strains which had ever before flowed even from beneath her fingers; it ceased with morning light; and as the day wore on it was found that Marian had fled during the night, and that Philip's organ had sounded its last strain—Lady Draye had shattered and silenced it forever. She never seemed to notice Marian's absence and no one dared to mention her name. Nothing was ever known certainly of her fate; it was supposed that she had joined her lover.

Years passed, and with each Lady Draye's temper grew fiercer and more malevolent. She never quitted her room unless on the anniversary of that day and night, when the tapping of her crutch and high-heeled shoes was heard for hours as she walked up and down the music-room, which was never entered save for this yearly vigil. The tenth anniversary came round, and this time the vigil was not unshared. The servants distinctly heard the sound of a man's voice mingling in earnest conversation with her shrill tones; they listened long, and at last one of the boldest ventured to look in, himself unseen. He saw a worn, travel-stained man; dusty, foot-sore, poorly dressed, he still at once recognised the hand-some, gay Philip of ten years ago. He held in his arms a little sleeping girl; her long curls, so like poor Marian's, strayed over his shoulder. He seemed to be pleading in that strange musical tongue for the little one; for as he spoke he lifted, O, so tenderly, the cloak which partly concealed her, and showed the little face, which he doubtless thought might plead for itself. The woman, with a furious gesture, raised her crutch to strike the child; he stepped quickly backward, stooped to kiss the little girl, then, without a word, turned to go. Lady Draye called on him to return with an imperious gesture, spoke a few words, to which he seemed to listen gratefully, and together they left the house by the window which opened on the terrace. The servants followed them, and found she led the way to the parsonage, which was at the time unoccupied. It was said that he was in some political danger as well as in deep poverty, and that she had hidden him here until she could help him to a better asylum. It was certain that for many nights she went to the parsonage and returned before dawn, thinking herself unseen. But one morning she did not come home; her people consulted together; her relenting towards Philip had made them feel more kindly towards her than ever before; they sought her at the parsonage and found her lying across its threshold dead, a vial clasped in her rigid fingers. There was no sign of the late presence of Philip and his child; it was believed she had sped them on their way before she killed herself. They laid her in a suicide's grave. For more than fifty years after the parsonage was shut up. Though it had been again inhabited no one had ever been terrified by the spectre I had seen; probably the Cedar Closet had never before been used as a bedroom.

Robert decided on having the wing containing the haunted room pulled down and rebuilt, and in doing so the truth of my story gained a horrible confirmation. When the wainscot of the Cedar Closet was removed a recess was discovered in the massive old wall, and in this lay mouldering fragments of the skeletons of a man and child!

There could be but one conclusion drawn; the wicked woman had imprisoned them there under pretence of hiding and helping them; and once they were completely at her mercy, had come night after night with unimaginable cruelty to gloat over their agony, and when that long anguish was ended, ended her odious life by a suicide's death. We could learn nothing of the mysterious painting. Philip was an artist, and it may have been his work. We had it destroyed, so that no record of the terrible story might remain. I have no more to add, save that but for those dark days left by Lady Draye as a legacy of fear and horror, I should never have known so well the treasure I hold in the tender, unwearying, faithful love of my husband—known the blessing that every sorrow carries in its heart, that

'Every cloud that spreads above
And veileth love, itself is love.'

WILL

Vincent O'Sullivan

*   *   *

Have the dead still power after they are laid in the earth? Do they rule us, by the power of the dead, from their awful thrones? Do their closed eyes become menacing beacons, and their paralysed hands reach out to scourge our feet into the paths which they have marked out? Ah, surely when the dead are given to the dust, their power crumbles into the dust!

Often during the long summer afternoons, as they sat together in a deep window looking out at the Park of the Sombre Fountains, he thought of these things. For it was at the hour of sundown, when the gloomy house was splashed with crimson, that he most hated his wife. They had been together for some months now; and their days were always spent in the same manner—seated in the window of a great room with dark oak furniture, heavy tapestry and rich purple hangings, in which a curious decaying scent of lavender ever lingered. For an hour at a time he would stare at her intensely as she sat before him—tall, and pale, and fragile, with her raven hair sweeping about her neck, and her languid hands turning over the leaves of an illuminated missal—and then he would look once more at the Park of the Sombre Fountains, where the river lay, like a silver dream, at the end. At sunset the river became for him turbulent and boding—a pool of blood; and the trees, clad in scarlet, brandished flaming swords. For long days they sat in that room, always silent, watching the shadows turn from steel to crimson, from crimson to grey, from grey to black.

If by rare chance they wandered abroad, and moved beyond the gates of the Park of the Sombre Fountains, he might hear one passenger say to another, 'How beautiful she is!' And then his hatred of his wife increased a hundredfold.

So he was poisoning her surely and lingeringly—with a poison more wily and subtle than that of Caesar Borgia's ring—with a poison distilled in his eyes. He was drawing out her life as he gazed at her; draining her veins, grudging the beats of her heart. He felt no need of the slow poisons which set fire to the brain; for his hate was a poison which he poured over her white body, till it would no longer have the strength to hold back the escaping soul. With exultation he watched her growing weaker and weaker as the summer glided by: not a day, not an hour passed that she did not pay toll to his eyes: and when in the autumn there came upon her two long faints which resembled catalepsy, he fortified his will to hate, for he felt that the end was at hand.

At length one evening, when the sky was grey in a winter sunset, she lay on a couch in the dark room, and he knew she was dying. The doctors had gone away with death on their lips, and they were left, for the moment, alone. Then she called him to her side from the deep window where he was seated looking out over the Park of the Sombre Fountains.

'You have your will,' she said. 'I am dying.'

'My will?' he murmured, waving his hands.

'Hush!' she moaned. 'Do you think I do not know? For days and months I have felt you drawing the life of my body into your life, that you might spill my soul on the ground. For days and months as I have sat with you, as I have walked by your side, you have seen me imploring pity. But you relented not, and you have your will; for I am going down to death. You have your will, and my body is dead; but my soul cannot die. No!' she cried, raising herself a little on the pillows: 'my soul shall not die, but live, and sway an all-touching sceptre lighted at the stars.'

'My wife!'

'You have thought to live without me, but you will never be without me. Through long nights when the moon is hid, through dreary days when the sun is dulled, I shall be at your side. In the deepest chaos illumined by lightning, on the loftiest mountain-top, do not seek to escape me. You are my bond-man; for this is the compact I have made with the Cardinals of Death.'

At the noon of night she died; and two days later they carried her to a burying-place set about a ruined abbey, and there they laid her in the grave. When he had seen her buried, he left the Park of the Sombre Fountains and travelled to distant lands. He penetrated the most unknown and difficult countries; he lived for months amid Arctic seas; he took part in tragic and barbarous scenes. He used himself to sights of cruelty and terror: to the anguish of women and children, to the agony and fear of men. And when he returned after years of adventure, he went to live in a house the windows of which overlooked the ruined abbey and the grave of his wife, even as the window where they had erewhile sat together overlooked the Park of the Sombre Fountains.

And here he spent dreaming days and sleepless nights—nights painted with monstrous and tumultuous pictures, and moved by waking dreams. Phantoms haggard and ghastly swept before him; ruined cities covered with a cold light edified themselves in his room; while in his ears resounded the trample of retreating and advancing armies, the clangor of squadrons, and noise of breaking war. He was haunted by women who prayed him to have mercy, stretching out beseeching hands—always women—and sometimes they were dead. And when the day came at last, and his tired eyes reverted to the lonely grave, he would soothe himself with some eastern drug, and let the hours slumber by as he fell into long reveries, murmuring at times to himself the rich, sonorous, lulling cadences of the poems in prose of Baudelaire, or dim meditative phrases, laden with the mysteries of the inner rooms of life and death, from the pages of Sir Thomas Browne.

On a night, which was the last of the moon, he heard a singular scraping noise at his window, and upon throwing open the casement he smelt the heavy odour which clings to vaults and catacombs where the dead are entombed. Then he saw that a beetle— a beetle, enormous and unreal—had crept up the wall of his house from the graveyard, and was now crawling across the floor of his room. With marvellous swiftness it climbed on a table placed near a couch on which he was used to lie, and as he approached, shuddering with loathing and disgust, he perceived to his horror that it had two red eyes like spots of blood. Sick with hatred of the thing as he was, those eyes fascinated him—held him like teeth. That night his other visions left him, but the beetle never let him go—nay! compelled him, as he sat weeping and helpless, to study its hideous conformation, to dwell upon its fangs, to ponder on its food. All through the night that was like a century—all through the pulsing hours—did he sit oppressed with horror gazing at that unutterable, slimy vermin. At the first streak of dawn it glided away, leaving in its trail the same smell of the charnel-house; but to him the day brought no rest, for his dreams were haunted by the abominable thing. All day in his ears a music sounded—a music thronged with passion and wailing of defeat, funereal and full of great alarums; all day he felt that he was engaged in a conflict with one in armour, while he himself was unharnessed and defenceless—all day, till the dark night came, when he observed the abhorred monster crawling slowly from the ruined abbey, and the calm, neglected Golgotha which lay there in his sight. Calm outwardly; but beneath perhaps—how disturbed, how swept by tempest! With trepidation, with a feeling of inexpiable guilt, he awaited the worm—the messenger of the dead. And this night and day were the type of nights and days to come. From the night of the new moon, indeed, till the night when it began to wane, the beetle remained in the grave; but so awful was the relief of those hours, the transition so poignant, that he could do nothing but shudder in a depression as of madness. And his circumstances were not merely those of physical horror and disgust: clouds of spiritual fear enveloped him: he felt that this abortion, this unspeakable visitor, was really an agent that claimed his life, and the flesh fell from his bones. So did he pass each day looking forward with anguish to the night; and then, at length, came the distorted night full of overwhelming anxiety and pain.

*　　*　　*

At dawn, when the dew was still heavy on the grass, he would go forth into the graveyard and stand before the iron gates of the vault in which his wife was laid. And as he stood there, repeating wild litanies of supplication, he would cast into the vault things of priceless value: skins of man-eating tigers and of leopards; skins of beasts that drank from the Ganges, and of beasts that wallowed in the mud of the Nile; gems that were the ornament of the Pharaohs; tusks of elephants, and corals that men had given their lives to obtain. Then holding up his arms, in a voice that raged against heaven he would cry: 'Take these, O avenging soul, and leave me in quiet! Are not these enough?'

And after some weeks he came to the vault again bringing with him a consecrated chalice studded with jewels which had been used by a priest at Mass, and a ciborium of the purest gold. These he filled with the rare wine of a lost vintage, and placing them within the vault he called in a voice of storm: 'Take these, O implacable soul and spare thy bond-man! Are not these enough?'

And last he brought with him the bracelets of the woman he loved, whose heart he had broken by parting with her to propitiate the dead. He brought a long strand of her hair, and a handkerchief damp with her tears. And the vault was filled with the misery of his heart-quaking whisper: 'O my wife, are not *these* enough?'

But it became plain to those who were about him that he had come to the end of his life. His hatred of death, his fear of its unyielding caress, gave him strength; and he seemed to be resisting with his thin hands some palpable assailant. Plainer and more deeply coloured than the visions of delirium, he saw the company which advanced to combat him: in the strongest light he contemplated the scenery which surrounds the portals of dissolution. And at the supreme moment, it was with a struggle far greater than that of the miser who is forcibly parted from his gold, with an anguish far more intense than that of the lover who is torn from his mistress, that he gave up his soul.

On a shrewd, grey evening in the autumn they carried him down to bury him in the vault by the side of his wife. This he had desired; for he thought that in no other vault however dark, would the darkness be quite still; in no other resting-place would he be allowed to repose. As they carried him they intoned a majestic threnody—a chant which had the deep tramp and surge of a triumphant march, which rode on the winds, and sobbed through the boughs of ancient trees. And having come to the vault they gave him to the grave, and knelt on the ground to pray for the ease of his spirit. *Requiem æternam dona ei, Domine!*

But as they prepared to leave the precincts of the ruined abbey, a dialogue began within the vault—a dialogue so wonderful, so terrible, in its nature, its cause, that as they hearkened they gazed at one another in the twilight with wry and pallid faces.

And first a woman's voice.

'You are come.'

'Yes, I am come,' said the voice of a man. 'I yield myself to you—the conqueror.'

'Long have I awaited you,' said the woman's voice. 'For years I have lain here while the rain soaked through the stones, and snow was heavy on my breast. For years while the sun danced over the earth, and the moon smiled her mellow smile upon gardens and pleasant things. I have lain here in the company of the worm, and I have leagued with the worm. You did nothing but what I willed; you were the toy of my dead hands. Ah, you stole my body from me, but I have stolen your soul from you!'

'And is there peace for me—now—at the last?'

The woman's voice became louder, and rang through the vault like a proclaiming trumpet. 'Peace is not mine! You and I are at last together in the city of one who queens it over a mighty empire. Now shall we tremble before the queen of Death.'

The watchers flung aside the gates of the vault and struck open two coffins. In a mouldy coffin they found the body of a woman having the countenance and the warmth of one who has just died. But the body of the man was corrupt and most horrid, like a corpse that has lain for years in a place of graves.

THE BRIDE
M. P. Shiel

* * *

They met at Krupp and Mason's, musical-instrument-makers, of Little Britain, E.C, where Walter had been employed two years, and then came Annie to typewrite, and be serviceable. They began to 'go out' together after six o'clock; and when Mrs Evans, Annie's mamma, lost her lodger, Annie mentioned it, and Walter went to live with them at No. 13 Culford Road, N.; by which time Annie and Walter might almost be said to have been engaged. His salary, however, was only thirty shillings a week.

He was the thorough Cockney, Walter; a well-set-up person of thirty, strong-shouldered, with a square brow, a moustache, and black acne-specks in his nose and pale face.

It was on the night of his arrival at No. 13 that he for the first time saw Rachel, Annie's younger sister. Both girls, in fact, were named 'Rachel'—after a much-mourned mother of Mrs Evans'; but Annie Rachel was called 'Annie', and Mary Rachel was called 'Rachel'. Rachel helped Walter at the handle of his box to the top-back room, and here, in the lamplight he was able to see that she was a tallish girl, with hair almost black, and with a sprinkling of freckles on her very white, thin nose, on the tip of which stood collected, usually, some little sweats. She was thin-faced, and her top teeth projected a little so that her lips only closed with effort, she not so pretty as pink-and-white little Annie, though one could guess, at a glance, that she was a person more to be respected.

143

'What do you think of him?' said Annie, meeting Rachel as she came down.

'He seems a nice fellow,' Rachel said: 'rather goodlooking. And strong in the back, you bet.'

Walter spent that evening with them in the area front room, smoking a foul bulldog pipe, which slushed and gurgled to his suction; and at once Mrs Evans, a dark old lady without waist, all sighs and lack of breath, decided that he was 'a gentlemanly, decent fellow'. When bed-time came he made the proposal to lead them in prayer; and to this they submitted, Annie having forewarned them that he was 'a Christian'. As he climbed to his room, the devoted girl found an excuse to slip out after him, and in the passage of the first floor there was a little kiss.

'Only one,' she said, with an uplifted finger.

'And what about his little brother, then?' he chuckled—a chuckle with which all his jokes were accompanied: a kind of guttural chuckle, which seemed to descend or stick straining in the throat, instead of rising to the lips.

'You go on,' she said playfully, tapped his cheek, and ran down. So Walter slept for the first night at Mrs Evans'.

On the whole, as time passed, he had a good deal of the society of the women: for the theatre was a thing abominable to him, and in the evenings he stayed in the underground parlour, sharing the bread-and-cheese supper, and growing familiar with the sighs of Mrs Evans over her once estate in the world. Rachel, the silent, sewed; Annie, whose relation with Walter was still unannounced, though perhaps guessed, could play hymn-tunes on the old piano, and she played. Last of all, Walter laid down the inveterate wet pipe, led them in prayer, and went to bed. Most mornings he and Annie set out together for Little Britain.

There came a day when he confided to her his intention to ask for a rise of 'screw', and when this was actually promised by His Terror, the Boss, there was joy in heaven, and radiance in futurity, and secret talks of rings, a wedding, 'a Home'. Annie felt herself not far from the kingdom of Hymen, and rejoiced. But nothing, as yet, was said at No. 13: for to Mrs Evans' past grandeurs thirty shillings a week was felt to be inappropriate.

The next Sunday, however, soon after dinner, this strangeness occurred: Rachel, the silent, disappeared. Mrs Evans called for her, Annie called, but it was found that she was not in the house, though the putting away of the dinner-things, her usual task, was only half accomplished. Not till tea-time did Rachel return. She was then cold, and somewhat sullen, and somewhat pale, her lips closing firmly over her projecting teeth. When timidly questioned—for her resentment was greatly feared—she replied that she had just been looking in upon Alice Soulsby, a few squares away, for a little chat: and this was the truth.

It was not, however, the whole truth; she had also looked in at the Church Lane Sunday School on her way: and this fact she guiltily concealed. For half an hour she had sat darkly at the end of the building in a corner, listening to the 'address'. This address was delivered by Walter. To this school every Sunday, after dinner, he put down the beloved pipe to go. He was, in fact, its 'superintendent'.

After this, the tone and temper of the little household rapidly changed, and a true element of hell was introduced into its platitude. It became, first of all, a question whether or not Rachel could be 'experiencing religion', a thing which her mother and Annie had never dreamt of expecting of her. Praying people, and the Salvationist, had always been the contempt of her strong and callous mind. But on Sunday nights she was now observed to go out alone, and 'chapel' was the explanation which she coolly gave. *Which* chapel she did not specify: but in reality it was the Newton Street Hall, at which Walter frequently exhorted and 'prayed'. In the Church Lane schoolroom there was prayer-meeting on Thursday evenings; and twice within one month Rachel sallied forth on Thursday evening—soon after Walter. The secret disease which preyed upon the poor girl could hardly now be concealed. At first she suffered bitter, solitary shame; sobbed in a hundred paroxysms; hoped to draw a veil over her infirmity. But her gash was too glaring. In the long Sabbath evenings of summer he preached at street corners, and sometimes secretly, sometimes openly, Rachel would attend these meetings, singing meekly with the rest the undivine hymns of the modern evangelist. In his presence, in the parlour, on other nights, she quietly sewed, hardly speaking. When, at 7 p.m., she heard his key in the front door her heart darted towards its master; when in the morning he flew away to business her universe was cinders.

'It's a wonder to me what's coming to our Rachel lately,' said

Annie in the train, coming home; 'you're doing her soul good, or something, aren't you?'

He chuckled, with slushy suction-sounds about the back of the tongue and molars.

'Oh, that be jiggered for a tale!' he said: '*she's* all right.'

'I know her better than you, you see. She's quite changed— since you've come. Looks to me as if she's having a touch of the blues, or something.'

'Poor thing! She wants looking after, don't she?'

Annie laughed, too: but less brutally, more uneasily.

Walter said: 'But she *oughtn't* to have the blues, if she's giving her heart to the Lord! People seem to think a Christian must be this and that. A Christian, if it comes to that, ought to be the jolliest fellow going!'

This was on a Thursday, the night of the Church Lane prayer-meeting, and Walter had only time to rush in at No. 13, wash his face, snatch his Bible, and be off. Rachel, for her part, must verily now have been badly bitten with the rabies of love, or she would have felt that to follow tonight, for the third time lately, could not fail to incur remark. But this consideration never even entered a mind now completely blinded and entranced by the personality of Walter. Through the day her work about the house had been rushed forward with this very object, and at the moment when he banged the door after him she was before her glass, dressing in blanched, intense and trembling flurry, and casting as she bent to give the last touches to her fringe, a look of bitterest hate at the projection of her lip above the teeth.

This night, for the first time, she waited in the chapel till the end of the service, and walked slowly homeward on the way which she knew that Walter would take; and he came striding presently, that morocco Bible in his hand, nearly every passage in which was neatly under-ruled in black and red inks.

'What, is that you?' he said, taking into his a hand cold with sweat.

'It is,' she answered, in a hard, formal tone.

'You don't mean to say you've been to the meeting?'

'I do.'

'Why, where were my eyes? *I* didn't see you.'

'It isn't likely that you would want to, Mr Teeger.'

'Go on—drop that! What do you take me for? I'm only too

glad! And I tell you what it is, Miss Rachel, I say to you as the Lord Jesus said to the young man: "Thou art not far from the kingdom of heaven."'

She was *in* it!—near him, alone, in a darkling square, yet suffering, too, in the flames of a passion such as perhaps consumes only the strongest natures.

She caught for support at his unoffered arm; and when he bent his steps straight homeward, she said trembling violently: 'I don't wish to go home as yet. I wish to have a little walk. Do you mind, Mr Teeger?'

'Mind, no. Come along, then,' and they went walking among an intricacy of streets and squares, he talking of 'the Work', and of common subjects. After half an hour, she was saying: 'I often wish I was a man. A man can say and do what he likes; but with a girl it's different. There's you, now, Mr Teeger, always out and about, having people listening to you, and that. I often wish I was only a man.'

'Oh, well, it all depends how you look at it,' he said. 'And, look here, you may as well call me Walter and be done.'

'Oh, I shouldn't think of *that*,' she replied. 'Not till—'

Her hand trembled on his arm.

'Well, out with it, why don't you?'

'Till—till we know something more definite about you—and Annie.'

He chuckled slushily, she now leading him fleetly round and round a square.

'Ah, you girls again!' he cried, 'been blabbing again like all the girls! It takes a bright man to hide much from them, don't it?'

'But there isn't much to hide in this case, as far as I can see—*is* there?'

Always Walter laughed, straining deep in the throat. He said: 'Oh, come—that would be telling, wouldn't it?'

After a minute's stillness, this treacherous phrase came from Rachel: 'Annie doesn't care for anyone, Mr Teeger.'

'Oh, come—that's rather a tall order, *any* one. *She's* all right.'

'But she *doesn't*. Of course, most girls are silly, and that, and like to get married—'

'Well, that's only nature, ain't it?'

This was a joke; and downward the laugh strained in his throat, like struggling phlegm.

'Yes, but they don't understand what love is,' said Rachel. 'They haven't an idea. They like to be married women, and have a husband, and that. But they don't know what love is—believe me! The men don't either.'

How she trembled!—her body, her dying voice—she pressing heavily upon him, while the moon triumphed now through cloud glaring a moment white on the lunacy of her ghostly face.

'Well, I don't know—I think *I* understand, lass, what it is,' he said.

'You don't, Mr Teeger!'

'How's that, then?'

'Because, when it takes you, it makes you—'

'Well, let's have it. You seem to know all about it.'

Now Rachel commenced to tell him what 'it' was—in frenzied definitions, and a power of expression strange for her. *It* was a lunacy, its name was Legion, it was possession by the furies; it was a spasm in the throat, and a sickness of the limbs, and a yearning of the eye-whites, and a fire in the marrow; it was catalepsy, trance, apocalypse; it was high as the galaxy, it was addicted to the gutter; it was Vesuvius, borealis, the sunset; it was the rainbow in a cesspool, St John plus Heliogabalus, Beatrice plus Messalina; it was a transfiguration, and a leprosy, and a metempsychosis, and a neurosis; it was the dance of the maenads, and the bite of the tarantula, and baptism in a sun: out poured the wild definition in simple words, but with the strife of one fighting for life. And she had not half done when he understood her fully; and he had no sooner understood her, than he was subdued, and succumbed.

'You don't mean to say—' he faltered.

'Ah, Mr Teeger,' she answered, 'there's none so blind as those who will not see.'

His arm stole round her shuddering body.

Everyone is said to have his failing; and this man, Walter, in no respect a man of strong mind, was certainly on his amatory side, most sudden, promiscuous, and infirm. And this tendency was, if anything, heightened by the quite sincere strain of his mind in the direction of 'spiritual things': for, under sudden temptation, back rushed his being, with the greater rigour, into its natural channel. On the whole, had he not been a Puritan, he would have been a Don Juan.

In an instant Rachel's weight was hanging upon his neck, he kissing her with passion.

After this she said to him: 'But you are only doing this out of pity, Walter. Tell the truth, you are in love with Annie?'

He, like Peter, tumbled at once into a fib. 'That's what *you* say!'

'You are,' she insisted, filled with the bliss of the fib.

'Bah! I'm not. Never was. *You* are the girl for me.'

When they went home, they entered the house at different times, she first, he waiting twenty minutes in the street.

The house was small, so the sisters slept together in the second-floor front room; Walter in the second-floor back; Mrs Evans in the first-floor back, the first-floor front being 'the drawing-room'. The girls, therefore, generally went to bed together: and that night, as they undressed, there was a row.

First, a long silence. Then Rachel, to say something, pointed to some new gloves of Annie's, asking: 'How much did you give for those?'

'Money and kind words,' replied Annie.

This was the beginning.

'Well, there's no need to be rude about it,' said Rachel. She was happy, in paradise, despised Annie that night.

'Still,' said Annie, after a silence of ten minutes before the glass, '*still*, I should never run after a man like that. I'd die first.'

'I haven't the least idea what you're talking about,' replied Rachel.

'You have. I should be *ashamed* of myself, if I were you.'

'Talk away. You're a little fool.'

'It's *you*. Throwing yourself at the head of a man who doesn't care for you. What *can* you call yourself?'

Rachel laughed—happily, yet dangerously.

'Don't bother yourself, my girl,' she said.

'Think of going out every night to meet a man in that way: look here, it's too disgusting of you, girl!'

'Is it?'

'You can't deny that you were with Mr Teeger tonight?'

'That I wasn't.'

'It's false! Anyone can see it by the joy in your face.'

'Well, suppose I was, what about it?'

'But a woman should be decent, I think; a woman should be

able to command her feelings, and not expose herself like that. Believe me, it gives me the creeps all over to think of.'

'Never mind, don't be jealous, my girl.'

The gentle Annie flamed!

'Jealous! of *you!*'

'There isn't any need, you know—not *yet.*'

'But I'm *not!* There never *will* be need! Do you take Mr Teeger for a raving lunatic? I should go and have some false teeth put in first if I were you!'

Thus did Annie drop to the rock-bed of vulgarity; but she knew it to be necessary in order to touch Rachel, as with a white-hot wire, on her very nerve of anguish, and, in fact, at these words Rachel's face resembled white iron, while she cried out, 'Never mind my teeth! It isn't the teeth a man looks at! A man knows a finely built woman when he sees her—not like a little dumpy podge!'

'Thank you. You are very polite,' replied Annie, browbeaten by an intensity fiercer than her own. 'But still, it's nonsense, Rachel, to talk of my being jealous of *you.* I knew **Mr Teeger** six months before you. And you won't know him much longer either, for I don't want to have mother disgraced here, and this is no fit place for him to lodge in. I can easily make him leave it soon—'

At this thing Rachel flew, with minatory palm over Annie's cheek, ready to strike. 'You *dare* do anything to make him go away! I'll tear your little—'

Annie winked, flinched, uttered a sob, no more fight left in her.

So for two weeks the situation lasted. Only, after that night, so intense grew the bitterness between the sisters, that Annie moved down to the first-floor back, sleeping now with Mrs Evans who dimly wondered. As for Walter, meanwhile, his heart was divided within him. He loved Annie; he was fascinated and mesmerised by Rachel. In another age and country he would have married both. Every day he came to a different resolve, not knowing what to do. One thing was evident—a wedding ring would be necessary, and he purchased one, uncertain for which of the girls.

'Look here, lass,' he said to Annie in the train, coming home, 'let us put a stop to this. The boss doesn't seem to be in a hurry about that rise of screw, so suppose we get spliced, and be done?'

'Privately?'

'Rather. Your ma and sister mustn't know—not just yet a while.'

'And you will still keep on living at the house?'

'Well, of course, for the time being.'

She looked up into his face and smiled. It was settled.

But two nights afterwards he met Rachel on his way home from prayer-meeting; at first was honest and distant; but then committed the incredible weakness of going with her for a walk among the squares, and ended by winning from her an easily granted promise of marriage, on the same terms as those arranged with Annie.

When, the next day at lunch-time, he put his foot on the threshold of the Registrar's office to give notice, he was still in a state of agonised indecision as to the name which he should couple with his own.

When the official said, 'Now the name of the other party?' Walter hesitated, shuffled with his feet, then answered:

'Rachel Evans.'

Not till he was again in the street did he remember that Rachel was the name of both the girls, and that liberty of choice between them still remained to him.

Now, from the day of 'notice' to the day of wedlock, an interval of twenty-one clear days must, by law, elapse, and Walter, though weak enough to inform both the sisters of the step he had taken, was careful to give them only a vague idea of the date fixed. His once clear conscience, meanwhile, was grievously troubled, his feet in a net; he feared to speak to God; and went drifting like flotsam on the river of chance.

And chance alone it was which at last cast him upon the land. The fifth day before the marriage was a Bank Holiday, and he had arranged with Rachel to go out with her that day to Hyde Park, she to wait for him at an arranged spot at two o'clock. At two, then, at a street-corner, stood Rachel waiting, twirling her parasol, walking a little, returning. Walter, however, did not appear, and what could have happened was beyond her divination. Had he misunderstood or missed her? Though incredible, it was the only thing to think. To Hyde Park, at any rate, she went alone, feeling desolate and *ennuyée*, in the vague hope of there meeting him.

What had happened was this: Walter had been halfway towards the rendezvous with Rachel, when he was met in the street by

Annie, who had gone to spend the day with a married friend at Stroud Green, but had returned, owing to the husband's illness. Seeing Walter, her face lit up with smiles.

'Harry's down with the influenza,' she said, 'so I couldn't stay and bore poor Ethel. Where are you going?'

For the first time since his 'conversion' twelve years before, Walter, with a high flush, now consciously lied.

'Only to the schoolroom,' he said, 'to hunt for something.'

'Well, I am open to be taken out, if any kind friend will be so kind,' she said fondly.

Now he had that morning vowed to himself to wed Rachel; and by this vow he now again vowed to be bound. All the more reason why, for the last time, he should 'take out' Annie.

'Come along, then, old girl,' he gaily said: 'where shall we go?'

'Let us go to Hyde Park,' said Annie. And to Hyde Park they went, Walter, ever and anon, stabbed by the bitter memory of waiting Rachel.

At five o'clock the two were walking along the north bank of the Serpentine westward towards a two-arched bridge, which is also pierced by a third narrow arch over the bank: to this narrow arch, since it was drizzling, they were making for shelter, when Rachel, a person of the keenest vision, sighted them from the south bank. She was frantic at once. Annie, who was supposed to be at Stroud Green! *What treachery!* This, then, was why . . . She ran panting along the bank, towards the bridge, then over it, northward, and now heard the two under the arch, who stood there talking—of the wedding. Unfortunately, just here is a block of masonry, which prevented Rachel from leaning directly over the arch to listen. Yet the necessity to hear was absolute: so she ran back clear of the masonry, and bent far over the parapet, outwards and sideways towards the arch, straining neck, body, ears, and anyone looking into those staring eyes *then* would have comprehended the doctrine of the Ferine Soul. But she was at a disadvantage, heard only murmurs, and—was that a kiss? Further and further forth she strained. And now suddenly, with a cry, she is in the water, where it is shallow near the bank. In the fall her head struck upon a stone in the mud.

For three days she screamed continuously the name of Walter, filling the street with it, calling him hers only. On the third night, in the midst of a frightful crisis of cries, she suddenly died.

'Oh, Rachel, don't say you are dead!' cried Annie over her.

The death occurred two days before the marriage-day, and on the next, Walter, well wounded, said to Annie: 'This knocks our little affair on the head, of course.'

Annie was silent. Then, with a pout, she said: 'I don't see why. After all, it was her own fault, entirely. Why should *we* suffer?'

For the feud between the sisters had become cruel as death; and it outlasted death: Annie, on the subject of Rachel and Walter, being no longer a gentle girl, but marble, without respect or pity.

And so, in spite of the trepidations and hesitancy of Walter, the marriage took place, even while Rachel lay stretched on the bed in the second-floor front of No. 13.

The ceremony did not, however, transpire without hitch and omen. It was necessary, first of all, for Walter to forewarn Annie that he had given notice of her to the Registrar by her second name of 'Rachel'—a mad-looking proceeding that was almost the cause of a rupture which nothing but Walter's most ardent pleadings could steer him clear of. At any rate it was to 'Rachel', and not to 'Annie' that he was, as a matter of fact, after all married.

After the ceremony, performed in their lunch-time, they returned to business together in Little Britain.

At ten-o'clock the same night, as he was going up to bed, she ran after him, and in the passage there was a long, furtive kiss—their last on earth.

'Twelve o'clock?' he whispered intensely.

She held up her forefinger. 'One!'

'Oh, say twelve!'

She did not answer, but drew her palm playfully across his cheek, meaning consent, for Mrs Evans was an inveterately heavy sleeper. He went up. And, careful to leave his door a little ajar, he extinguished his candle, and went to bed. In the apartment nearby lay stark in the dark—with learned, eternal eyelids and drowsy brow—the dead.

Walter could not but think of this presence close at hand. 'Well, poor girl!' he sighed. 'Poor Rachel! Well, well. His way is in the sea, after all, and His path in the Great Deep, and His footsteps are not known.' Then he thought of Annie—the little wife! But instead of Annie, there was Rachel. The two women fought vehemently for his thought—and ever the dead was stronger than the living . . . Instead of Annie there was Rachel—and again Rachel.

At last he could hear twelve strike from a steeple, and sat up in bed, listening eagerly for the door to open, or a footfall on the floor.

A little American clock ticked in the room; and in the flue of the chimney was a sough and chant just audible.

Suddenly she was intensely with him, filling the chamber—from nowhere. He had heard no footstep, no opening of the door: yet certainly, she was with him *now*, all suddenly, close to him, over him, talking breathlessly to him.

His first sensation was a shuddering which strongly shook him from head to foot, like the shuddering of Russian cold. She held him down by the shoulders; was stretched at length on the bed, over him; and the room seemed full of a rustling and rushing, very strange, like starched muslins rushing out in stormy agitation. She was speaking, too, to him *in breathless haste*, whimpering a secret gibberish which whimpered like a pup for passion—about love and its definition, and about the soul, and the worm, and Eternity, and the passion of death, and the nuptials of the tomb, and the lust and hollowness of the void. And he, too, was speaking, whispering through his pattering teeth, saying: 'Sh-h-h, Rachel—Annie, I mean—sh-h-h, my girl—your ma will hear! Rachel, don't—sh-h-h, now!' But even while he kept up this 'sh-h-h, dear—sh-h-h, now,' he was conscious of the invasion of a strange rage, of such a strength as if energy was being vehemently pumped into him from some behemoth omnipotence. The form above him he could hardly discern, the room was so dark, but he felt that her garment was flowing forth from her neck in a continuous flutter, with the rustling of the starch of a thousand shrouds, like the outflow of a pennant in wind; and the quivering gauze seemed now to swell and fill the chamber, and now to sink again to the size of woman. And ever the rhapsody of love and death went on, mixed with the chattered 'Sh-h-h, Rachel—Annie, I mean,' of Walter; till, suddenly, he was involved in an embrace *so* horrible, felt himself encompassed by a might so intolerable, that his soul fainted within him. He sank back; thought span and failed in darkness beneath the spell of that lullaby; he muttered, 'Receive my spirit . . .'

After two days Walter, still unconscious, died. His disfigured body they placed in a grave not far from Rachel's.

ENCOUNTER AT NIGHT

Mary Frances McHugh

*   *   *

Dublin was growing deserted; only an odd car slid by in the dark, rainy night, for the second of its passing throwing a dazzle on the shiny pavements and lighting up the shuttered shops. Figures would pass, hurrying by with hunched shoulders—but less and less frequently.

Tom Donovan and his three friends scarcely felt the rain. They were hot and happy and bemused. All that each of them wanted was somehow to continue talking and drinking and smoking in genial company . . . But Jim, the red-haired barman at Flynn's, had gradually edged them out into the night, and bolted the doors against them. There was nothing for it but to go home.

'Take care of yourself, Joe!'

'Well, goodnight, boys!'

'Take care—see you tomorrow.'

The milk of human kindness flowed in them, and they patted one another's backs affectionately again and again before each went his separate way. Donovan, the shiftless poet, was left standing on the pavement, last and lonely. Slowly there faded from his face its smile of convivial bliss, and into his sobering mind crept back those thoughts which now, with the fleeting years, possessed him more and more in his solitary moments.

Wretched, killing thoughts. No, not thoughts—not thoughts, but feelings—or one feeling only, corroding unhappiness. A sense that life was vain and empty, with comfort nowhere—not even in drinking, in friendship, or in love. If even he knew friendship or love! A certainty that never, during all his existence, even when he had been young and gay and roistering, had he known ease: always a shadow had been lurking at his elbow. And it whispered to him that he was a fool to go on with the sham from day to day, that there was only one solution to everything: a knife or a rope for his throat.

Cruel memories came thronging. He saw a miserable, beaten peasant child: himself. All that child had really known was suffering, though the man had made sweet lilting songs of a boy, barefooted, in the West, birds'-nesting or tickling for trout in a mountain stream. The boy had been there, the sun, the stream, the idyllic sky, the irrational light-heartedness of childhood. These were the stuff of his verse—but not the harsh home, the pain and puzzled grief, the cold and hunger which had been more true and near. These things had made him!—they were with him even now.

Later, there was the man. A poet he was now, praised and wondered at for the clear innocency of his songs, toys fashioned for the cultured mind by a queer bohemian fellow. That he was so different from his poetry merely gave it zest. He knew this, and cultivated his oddity; and it was partly to curry favour with his admirers that he drank and sang his way through Europe without a word of any language but his own. Here, standing on a Dublin pavement in the night, he recalled the troubadour adventure and shivered—not because the steely rain was stinging his face and sending cold arrows through his clothing. No; but because from those wanderings from which he had so triumphantly returned he could now remember only a haunting horror. He evoked without willing it a night in Russia, when he lay in a country tavern with his familiar spirit beside him. There, in a big common room, several poor travellers slept about the stove. The air was humid with their breath and the odorous damp of their clothing, and the windows were sealed to blindness by the snow outside. In the yard there suddenly arose the commotion of a sledge being unharnessed; a bulky figure stepped into the room and looked stealthily around at the sleepers and fixedly at him, Donovan, before flinging itself likewise down in a corner. Donovan through half-closed eyes saw the stranger's Mongolian face, and as though he were a child it smote him with its mystery of a locked mind, of a race other than and alien to his own. There was no reason for his sudden panic of fear, or for the anguish of loneliness which overcame him then. It was simply part of the encompassing oppression of the world to his soul, driving him whither he knew not.

He tossed his head, heedless of the rain, appealing to the sky above him to protect and save. There must be rest somewhere, a cooling of this fever: why should he, more than other men, be so tormented? Why could he not be like little Terry Shaughnessy, caring nothing for anyone, whether drunk or sober, in funds or out of them? Now, there was an idea! Why go back, in this mood and in this weather, to his cold room and unwelcoming bed, when Terry would be glad enough for him to drop in for a smoke and a talk? He'd be there, sure enough, in his attic in Eustace Street. He wouldn't be in bed. Who ever heard of little Terry being in bed? He'd have a warm fire, and maybe a taste of something— 'one for the worms,' as he called it . . . Donovan turned towards Eustace Street.

He trotted along mechanically, now thinking cheerfully of himself and Terry. They were the only bachelors among the boys— and taking it all in all, he'd swear they were as well off like that. He thought of Ned Buckley's wife, and grinned to himself. A nice exhibition she made of the poor man, running to his newspaper office or writing to the editor when she wanted money. Ned was a good sort—but what kind of man was he to put up with that?

Now, if any woman tried to manage *him*—! Or Terry: he'd swear Terry would know how to deal with her, too. Keep a firm hand. That was it.

Yet, maybe—Terry as well as himself—in their hearts they'd like to have a home, and a woman waiting for them, and children. Maybe they'd die in the workhouse, no one caring enough for them to follow them to the grave . . . At these sad thoughts Donovan's mouth turned down again behind his coat collar, and he felt nearly dismal enough to cry. But resolutely he clung to the advantages of his state. He was his own master, anyway. He could drop in on Terry like this, tonight, and Terry be welcome to drop in on him, any hour he liked.

The rain beat on his face, stood in tears on his eyelashes till the street lamps carried a halo, each of them. Then he blinked and shook his head, and the long, deserted street shone straight before him again. A clock struck twelve. Ah, here was Terry's door. God, it was good to get in out of the rain!

The door stood ajar. That saved ringing the bell. Probably someone had left it like that on purpose—goodness knew how many lived in the old rookery. Not a glimmer of light. But Donovan felt his way to the banisters, gripped them, and mounted, cautiously counting the stairs.

Terry's door was opposite the fourth turn. Two . . . three . . . The next one . . . *Mother of God, what was that?*

Someone, coming out of the darkness, had struck him softly. A blow of a doubled-up fist in the face. Like a joke, by the Lord! But where had the fellow got to?

'Who's that?' called out Donovan, his voice a little startled in the night. 'Who's there? What the blazes are you doing.?'

There was no answer. Donovan crouched a moment in the darkness, very still, then changed his walking-stick to the other hand. But he must have been flustered, for his fingers didn't catch on it, and down it went clattering against the uncarpeted stairs, stopping once, clattering again, staying finally where it was. He stopped and groped, but thought better of going back for it. He stared about him and in the blackness thought he saw a solider patch, a man facing him a couple of steps up. That was the man who had struck him. But why on earth didn't he say something?

'Who's there?' he shouted again. 'Speak up, whoever you are!'

There was no answer, so he stepped forward boldly. But again someone pushed him—pushed him so plainly, as though with a playful gentleness, that he could feel the woollen jacket of the shoulder thrust against him. As in indignant alarm he tried to grasp it, it silently eluded him, moving soundlessly, eerily, out of reach.

Donovan's blood crept in his veins, and his heart seemed to lunge downwards in his body. Suddenly he wished he felt steadier, that he hadn't had so many drinks. Then he thought instinctively how another good stiff whisky would hearten him—yes, give him fire to tell this sly fellow, whoever the hell he was, what he thought of him.

He paused and gasped, listening with all his ears. Not a sound could he catch; and swiftly changing mood, convinced that it was only some silly trick being played on him, he became wildly angry.

'Come on!' he shouted, his excited voice falling back to the cadence of his native West. 'Come on, you puppy! Come on, you coward you, if you're a man at all, and I'll wrastle you in the Connemara fashion!'

He bent down over his right knee in an attitude of defence. 'I'll fight you! I'll wrastle you!' he repeated belligerently.

For a few seconds he held up his fists, awaiting his assailant. But the latter did not move. Then, like a bull, Donovan made to rush up the stairs. *Ah!*—With a soft thud he struck his head into the stomach of the lurking enemy. The invisible man, silent and unshocked, moved stealthily away.

But Donovan followed him, and as he did so was surprised to find the other coming towards him. He flung away caution and grasped his man about the body. Something rigid but yielding, human yet cold, lay unprotestingly within his arms. He released it and stepped back, weak and shuddering.

It swung—it hung . . . Ah, God!

Donovan recoiled, as sober as at morning. For a full minute he waited where he stood, overwhelmed with a nameless dread. Then he struck a match and, peering up, saw above him the blackened face of little Terry Shaughnessy, hanging from his attic banisters . . .

www.ingramcontent.com/pod-product-compliance
Lightning Source LLC
Chambersburg PA
CBHW030341030726
47499CB00003B/857